❧ *ESCAPE FROM ESHGORIN* ❧

He was pursued by the king's men. There was a price on his head. He had no food, no money, and nowhere to hide. His only companion was a mythical creature —a baby dragon, whom he had promised to protect and care for. Together they must find safety, in a world of barbarians and savages. This is the tale of their travels, seeking shelter, fleeing the soldiers of the king of Eshgorin. It is a strange, moving story of survival.

THE
SWORD SMITH

ELEANOR ARNASON

CONDOR

NEW YORK

THE SWORD SMITH

CONDOR

Printing History
CONDOR edition published May 1978

ISBN 0-89516-028-5
Library of Congress Catalog Number: 78-52972

Printed in the United States of America

CONDOR PUBLISHING COMPANY, INC.
521 Fifth Avenue
New York, N.Y. 10017

THE SWORD SMITH, FOR RUTH BERMAN &
DEVRA LANGSAM, WITH THE CARAVAN

WITH THE CARAVAN

A little after sunset he came in sight of the town. He reined his horse. Ahead of him the road went down into a wide valley, surrounded by low wooded hills. The town was at the valley's center: a little cluster of dimly glowing lights. A short distance from the town was a second, smaller cluster of lights, probably a caravan's camp fires. Nargri, who'd been sleeping curled up in the big saddle bag, raised her head and said, "What're you doing, Limper?"

"I was thinking those people down there might've heard about me."

"That doesn't seem likely to me," Nargri said. "We're a long way from Eshgorin, and you know the saying—what's big news in one home is no news in another."

"That's a dragon saying," Limper said, "and dragons don't travel much. Men do. And don't forget the king of Eshgorin is offering money for me. News about money is the kind of news people remember."

"You keep talking about that money the king's offering for you," Nargri said.

Limper grinned. "I know I'm worth something to somebody. That's more than many people can say."

Nargri said, "Are you going down there or not?"

"No." He turned off the road and went some distance from it, then made camp in a hollow where his campfire would be hidden. He had nothing to eat except a loaf of stale bread, which he divided with Nargri, and nothing to drink except water from the spring. The night was cold, but he didn't want to build a big fire. Nargri slept curled up next to him, covered by his cloak.

The next day was bright and cloudless. There was no more food, so he and Nargri had water for breakfast. It was cool in the hollow, in the shadow of the trees, but once they got out into the sunlight Limper felt hot. He circled the town and came back to the road on the other side of the valley, then followed the road eastward. The land flattened out, and there were fewer and fewer trees. A little before noon he came to where the steppe began. Ahead of him there was nothing except brown grass, the narrow caravan road, and the bright blue sky, cloudless from one horizon to the other. He stopped where a tree grew beside the road, dismounted and tied the horse's reins to the tree trunk.

"What now?" Nargri asked.

"Haven't you dragons heard about the herding peoples?"

"No," Nargri said. "To us, all men are more or

less alike. We've never bothered to learn how to distinguish the different breeds."

"The herding peoples live on the steppe. There are two kinds: the savage tribes that kill travelers and set their skulls up on poles outside their villages, and the civilized tribes that capture travelers and sell them to slave traders. We'll be safer on the steppe with traveling companions." He settled himself in the shade. Nargri climbed out of the saddle bag and sat crouched on the saddle. She was dappled with sunlight, and her dark grey scales shimmered. Limper looked at her a moment, then shut his eyes and dozed.

A little after noon Nargri said, "Something's coming." He stood and stretched. There was a cloud of dust on the road to the west. He watched it for a while, then said, "They're moving too slowly to be soldiers."

"You don't really think the king's going to send an army after you, do you?" Nargri asked.

"No, but I don't like soldiers." He untied the horse, mounted and rose toward the dust.

When he got closer he saw it was a caravan: a long line of horses carrying big packs with drivers walking beside them, and guards armed with lances riding alongside. When he was close enough to hear the drivers cursing, three horsemen came forward to meet him. One was little and dark and dressed like one of the herding peoples in a jacket and loose pants. The other two wore the same kind of pants, but they had mail shirts instead of jackets, and they wore metal helmets of the kind made in the southern cities. One of these men had a lance. The other had a bow. "What do you want?" the man with the lance asked.

Limper said, "Company. I don't want to cross the steppe alone."

They looked him over. "Very well," the man with the lance said. "What do you want us to call you?"

"Heshkya Atthal."

"I'm the caravan master, Yagoreb," the man with the lance said. He nodded toward the man with the bow. "That's Norem Archer, the captain of the caravan guards."

They turned then and rode back to the caravan, Limper riding with them.

That night the caravan camped beside the Great River at a spot where another smaller river came into it. The ground was marshy and the air full of insects. Limper bought a loaf of bread and a jar of wine from one of the drivers, then gave half the loaf to Nargri, who was in the saddlebag. He sat down close to one of the fires, ate the bread and drank the wine and listened to the drivers tell tales about the good times they'd had with the girls in the last town they'd been in. After a while Nargri climbed out of the saddlebag and came over to him.

One of the drivers said, "What's that?"

Limper said, "A dragon."

"Small, isn't it?" another driver said.

"She's still young, and dragons grow more slowly than we do."

"It's cold out here," Nargri said softly, so the drivers wouldn't hear her. "And I'm not going to sleep in a bag full of bread crumbs."

Limper opened his cloak. She curled up beside him, and he covered her with the cloak. He lay down a little later. By that time Nargri was asleep. He disturbed her, and she stirred and hissed. He put his arm around her. After that she was quiet.

The next day they went east along the Great

River. On every side the land was flat all the way to the horizon. The sky was cloudless. Limper wore a broad brimmed hat, but still his face got sunburned where his beard didn't protect it, and the back of his neck got sunburned too. They traveled east and north for ten days, and there was no trouble of any kind. Then, the evening of the tenth day, Nargri said, "Yagoreb looks at you a lot. He looks to me like a man trying to make up his mind about something."

"Damn his beady eyes." After a moment Limper said, "I don't think he'll do anything till we're closer to Hwara. I'm not likely to leave the caravan while we're in the country of the herding people."

Two days later, in the evening, after they'd made camp, a driver who was nicknamed Hog came to him and said, "I think you're in trouble, Heshkya."

"I'm not surprised," Limper said. "What kind?"

"I heard Yagoreb talking to Norem Archer. He said you were somebody called Limper, and you were worth a lot of money. Who would pay money for you?"

Limper shrugged. "Every man is valuable to somebody, his mother if nobody else. Thanks for telling me."

"Yaroreb has enough money already," Hog said. "Why should he make more?"

After Hog left him, he sat a while looking at the camp fire. At last Nargri said, "Well?"

"It's time to get out." Then he said, "I wish I had a better horse. That nag of mine would have a hard time outrunning a donkey."

That night he had trouble getting to sleep. In the end he stayed awake. Hog was lying close to him. Most nights Hog slept restlessly and muttered in his sleep, but this night he was still and silent.

When Nargri woke up the next morning Limper told her, "Stay close to me."

They ate breakfast, then Limper went to where the horses were tethered, his cloak over one shoulder. Nargri followed him. The sky was beginning to lighten in the east, but he could still see stars overhead, and it was still hard to make out the horses or the scouts who were beginning to saddle up. Nargri bumped against Limper's leg, and he stopped and bent to fiddle with his boot. Nargri said softly, "Hog's watching you, and so is Norem Archer."

Limper said, "The scout nearest us—get behind him and bite him."

"All right."

He straightened up and went over to the scout. "It's a cold morning."

The scout grunted and checked his saddle girths. Limper looked around quickly. He saw Norem Archer moving away from the campfires toward the horses, and he saw Nargri, barely visible, coming up behind the scout. "How much longer—" Limper started to say. Nargri leaped onto the scout's leg, digging her claws in and biting the scout on the back of the thigh. The scout yelled. Limper grabbed the horse's reins out of the scout's hands and shoved him back, then mounted. The scout moved toward him. Limper got his foot out of the stirrup and kicked him in the chest. The scout stumbled backward and fell. Limper yelled, "Nargri," then leaned down and grabbed her up when she ran to him. He kicked the horse, and the horse started forward. He looked back and saw Norem Archer running toward him, bow in hand. He kicked the horse again and said to Nargri, "Hold onto the saddle horn." Then he let go of her. With one hand he guided the horse between the other horses. With the other hand he pulled his sword out of its scabbard. A scout on horseback got in front of him. Limper brought his sword up, and the scout yanked his horse back out of the way. Limper passed him and was clear of the horses. Ahead of him was the dark steppe and the grey sky. He was just starting to grin when his horse grunted, staggered and started to fall. He jumped free, coming down on his bad leg. He rolled over, then scrambled to his feet. His bad leg hurt. He'd let go of his sword when he hit the ground, and he couldn't see it. He shouted, "Nargri, run."

He looked around and couldn't see her. The horse was about fifteen feet from him, lying on its side in the long grass. Men were running toward him. He took a couple of steps. His bad leg hurt so much that he could barely walk. He stopped and stood still, waiting for the men. The first one to get to him was Norem Archer. He was still holding his bow, and he had an arrow in his other hand. Limper spread his hands to show he was weaponless and said, "Did you shoot the horse?"

"That's certainly what I was trying to do, and it looks as if I succeeded."

"You're better with a bow than I thought," Limper said.

Then the scout came up. He went to his horse and looked at it, then said, "You owe me a horse, Norem."

"Ask Heshkya to pay you," Norem said. "I wouldn't have shot the horse if he hadn't tried to run off on it."

"Will you pay me, Heshkya?" the scout asked.

"I don't have anything to pay you with except my horse and my sword," Limper said.

"I've seen your horse. I'd like a look at your sword."

"It's somewhere in the grass," Limper said.

The scout started looking around. By this time other men had come up, and a couple of them helped the scout look. After a moment or two one of these found the sword and gave it to the scout. "I can't see it here," the scout said. He started back toward the campfires.

"Come on," Norem said to Limper, and they went after the scout. Limper was walking slowly, dragging his bad leg.

When they got to the closest of the campfires, the scout stopped and looked at the sword. The blade had been made out of steel from the east and had a rippling pattern on it. The hilt was made in a northern style, and the guard and pommel were in-laid with silver and copper. "It looks as if it's worth as much as my horse was."

Limper said, "It's worth a lot more. You aren't likely to get your hands on a better sword."

After that they took Limper to Yagoreb, who was squatting down beside one of the campfires, eating his breakfast. He looked up at Limper. After a moment he said, "Put him on a horse. You'd better tie him to it. He's lost one horse already. Norem, tell a couple of your men to stay with him and see that he doesn't come to any harm." Then Yagoreb picked up a loaf of bread, tore off a piece and bit into it.

Norem Archer looked around, then pointed at two men and said, "You two watch him."

The guards came over to Limper. One was short and fat, his belly hanging out over his belt, barely covered by his shirt. The other guard was thin and looked as if he'd been handsome when he was younger, but now there were lines around his mouth, and the skin under his eyes was puffy and dark. He'd shaved within the last day or two; and his hair was carefully combed. His clothes looked pretty clean. His shirt was embroidered with gold thread around the neck. The thread was tarnished, and the shirt had been mended in several places. Limper looked the two of them over, then shrugged. "What do you two call yourselves?"

The short fat guard said, "I'm called the Geshurite, and this fellow here is Pretty Boy." He waved at the other guard.

They took him to where his horse was tethered and saddled the horse. After he'd mounted, they tied his hands to the saddlehorn. Then the guards got their horses. By this time the scouts had ridden off. The guards were all mounted, and some of the drivers were beginning to lead their horses out of camp. They rode to the front of the caravan, the guards on either side of Limper. The east was pink, and the morning star was the only star still in sight. Soon the sun came up. It was another bright, cloudless day. After a while, Limper asked Pretty Boy, "Did Nargri get away?"

"Nargri?"

The Geshurite said, "He means that big lizard of his. Some of the scouts were going looking for it."

"Bad luck to them," Limper said. His bad leg was still bothering him. He shifted in his saddle, trying to ease the pain.

The scouts caught up with the caravan at noon. One of the scouts who'd stayed with the caravan shouted something in the language of the herding people. They shook their heads.

The Geshurite said, "It looks as if bad luck is what they had."

Later in the day Pretty Boy asked, "That lizard, is it really a dragon?"

Limper nodded.

"I thought dragons were big and spit fire."

"Nargri's a child. A full grown dragon is the same size as a full grown man. As for spitting fire, that story must've started because wherever there are dragons there's fire. They're great smiths. Their deep homes are always full of smoke and the sound of hammers."

"I never heard that dragons were smiths," Pretty Boy said.

"Where do you think the gold in dragonhoards come from?"

"I thought they stole it from men."

Limper shook his head. "Men steal it from dragons. Dragons mine the gold, refine it and shape it. There are no more skillful smiths anywhere, though I think men make more lovely things. Dragons are more interested in ingenuity than in loveliness."

"You know a lot about dragons," the Geshurite said.

Limper nodded.

"My father used to say, every man knows a lot about something."

"That may well be," Limper said.

A little before sunset the caravan stopped, and they made camp by the side of the Great River. The guards untied Limper so he could dismount. Once on the ground he stretched, then rubbed his wrists. Close by him he could see the river, brown water sliding between dull green reeds. There was a big white bird, a stork or a crane, standing on a sandbar at the river's center. All at once it spread its wings and flapped up into the sky.

"Come on and eat," Pretty Boy said.

Limper sighed and turned toward the campfire.

After he'd eaten, they tied his hands and feet. He soon found out that there was no way he could sit or lie so that he was comfortable. At last he said, "Why do you have to tie my legs? I'm not fleet footed in the best of times, and my leg's been hurting ever since I fell on it this morning. I'm not about to run away from you."

After a moment Pretty Boy shrugged, then untied the rope around Limper's ankles. A while later Yagoreb came over. Limper looked up at him and asked, "Who do you think I am?"

"Before we set out, I heard about a man called Limper. They say the king of Eshgorin will pay well to get ahold of him."

"We're a long way from Eshgorin," Limper said.

"That isn't my problem. We're only three days from Hwara, and the king has an ambassador there. I'll sell you to him."

"Would it make any difference to you if I said I'm not Limper?"

"If you aren't Limper, then why'd you run when Hog told you I thought you were Limper?"

"Give me some time, and I'll find an answer for that."

"All right," Yagoreb said. He looked to the Geshurite. "If you aren't going to tie his legs, you'll have to take turns watching him during the night."

"We'll tie his feet before we go to sleep," Pretty Boy said.

Yagoreb left. After he was gone the Geshurite said, "How much is the king willing to pay for you?"

Limper said, "The last I heard, the king was offering a hundred pieces of gold for Limper."

"That much? The richest man in Geshur didn't have that much money, though he had enough to marry off six daughters, each one uglier than the last. Even the one with warts got a good husband."

"What'd you do to make him want you so badly?" Pretty Boy asked.

"You've never heard of Limper?" Limper asked. "I thought he was a famous man."

Pretty Boy shook his head.

"He's a master smith. He used to work for the king of Eshgorin."

"What'd he—you—do?" Pretty Boy asked.

"He left Eshgorin."

"Is that all?" the Geshurite asked.

"Do you think there are so many good smiths around that the king can afford to lose one?"

"That's true," the Geshurite said. "The old smith in Geshur had no sons. When he died, it was two years before we found a new smith, and he wasn't much good."

A little while later Limper saw Hog by another one of the campfires and called to him, "Come over here, Hog."

Hog looked over at him, then looked away and stayed where he was.

"He's tied up," the Geshurite called. "He can't hurt you."

After a moment Hog came over and said, "What do you want?"

Limper said, "There are a lot of stories about

what happens to men who sell their fellows. The one I like best says after they die they go to the bottom of a deep hole. There are snakes above them that drip poison on them, and the poison burns like fire."

"That's a good story," the Geshurite said.

Hog said, "I owed you nothing," and walked away.

Pretty Boy spat on the ground.

A little while later the guards retied Limper's feet, and he lay down to sleep. He woke from time to time during the night to turn from one side to the other. When he woke the last time, at dawn, his arms ached, and his wrists and hands were numb. He sat up. The Geshurite was lying close by him. Limper put his feet against the Geshurite's side and pushed. The Geshurite rolled half way over, then said, "Huh," and sat up. Limper said, "Untie me. I think my hands are going to fall off. If I were Limper, and I'm not saying I am, the king of Eshgorin wouldn't want to get me back without my hands."

The Geshurite grunted, then got up, came over and untied Limper. He sat awhile rubbing his wrists and arms and clenching and unclenching his hands.

After that Pretty Boy got up and went to get them breakfast. After they'd eaten, the guards saddled their three horses. They tied Limper's hands to the saddle horn, as they had done the day before.

It was another clear day. The caravan trail left the Great River and went straight east across the steppe. In the early afternoon the land they crossed began to rise. Late in the afternoon they saw a band of riders a long way off. The Geshurite shaded his eyes and watched them a while, then said, "Herding people."

"It seems strange to me that we haven't seen them before," Limper said.

Pretty Boy said, "The scouts say most of them are still far north of here in the summer country."

Soon after that the caravan stopped for the night. There were more guards than usual keeping watch at the edges of the camp. The drivers kept looking around and stopping their conversations to listen. But nothing happened. The herding people never showed up.

While they were eating, Limper said to the Geshurite and Pretty Boy, "A hundred pieces of gold is a lot of money. Haven't you thought of getting ahold of it for yourselves?"

The Geshurite said, "If we took you back to Eshgorin, we'd have to cross the steppe by ourselves and risk meeting the herding people. Besides, it's a long trip, and there'd be only the two of us watching you. You might get away from us before we got to Eshgorin."

"What about Hwara?" Limper asked.

Pretty Boy shook his head. "If Yagoreb found us gone, he'd send a man to Hwara to say we'd stolen you from him. Then we'd end up in court. And when have poor men won a court case against a rich man?"

"I don't suppose you'd let me get away."

The Geshurite shook his head. "We'd be out of a job, if we did that. Pretty Boy might find a rich widow to take care of him, but I wouldn't."

"I just thought I'd ask," Limper said. "Norem Archer knew what he was doing when he picked you two to watch me."

They finished eating, and Pretty Boy tied Limper up. That night he had trouble sleeping again, and he woke up the Geshurite some time before dawn and told him, "Untie me."

"Go back to sleep," the Geshurite said.

"I can't. My arms hurt," Limper said.

The Geshurite swore and got up and untied him.

They were on the steppe for one more day. In the evening the caravan made camp in sight of the mountains. The next day before noon, they came to the foothills. The caravan trail went beside a narrow river, low at this time of year and full of rocks. There were poplars in the valley and pine trees on the upper slopes, and the air smelled of pine. Early in the afternoon they passed below the first watch towers. They were tall and round, built out of big blocks of stone. Late in the afternoon they came to Hwara, which was a high walled city on top of the hill. Beyond the hill were cliffs where the Iburi Pass began. In front of the hill was a flat place, enclosed by a second outer wall. The wall was built of stone and had watch towers along it. Where they were—on the trail beside the river—they were in shadow, but the city and its fortifications were sunlit. Limper saw metal glittering on top of the wall and the watch towers and the gate. He said, "They don't trust strangers, do they?"

Pretty Boy grinned. "They don't trust each other in Hwara. Wait till you see the city. Every house has bars on the windows and a strong lock on the door."

The caravan went in through the gate and made camp below the city, inside the outer wall. Beggers and pedlars and cheap whores came down

out of the town. The drivers bought wine and got
drunk and listened to the beggers tell their hard-
luck stories. Then the drivers began to go off with
the whores into the darkness beyond the campfires. Pretty Boy and the Geshurite bought a jug of
wine and shared it with Limper. They swore at
him because they had to stay put and watch him.

"You can go for all I care," Limper said. "And I
hope you get the whore's disease."

Pretty Boy shrugged. "There'll be time enough
for that."

"Watch it," the Geshurite said.

Pretty Boy hid the jug under his cloak. Limper
looked up and saw Yagoreb coming toward them.
There was another man with him, short and dark,
like most of the men of Eshgorin. He wore a red
gown, fastened by a belt with a big gold buckle,
and he had gold bracelets on both his arms. He
and Yagoreb stopped and looked at Limper. After a
moment Yagoreb said, "Well?"

The short man said, "He might be Limper, and
then again he might not. I never saw Limper when
I was in Eshgorin."

Yagoreb said, "From what I heard, Limper is a
northerner and has hair so fair that it looks white,
and he's lame in one leg. Well, this fellow is a
northerner and white haired, and he limps."

"I haven't seen him limp," the short man said.

"Get up and walk," Yagoreb told Limper.

The short man said, "There must be more than
one northerner who limps. As for the white hair,
most of them have white or yellow hair."

Limper said, "Why don't you ask me if I'm this
fellow?"

The short man asked, "Are you?"

"No."

Yagoreb said, "You aren't going to take his word, are you?"

The short man shook his head. "If he is Limper, he'd certainly say he isn't, since if he says he is he'll be sent back to Eshgorin. So it's clear that I can't take his word."

"Then why'd you ask me?" Limper said.

"Do you know any way to find out whether or not he's Limper?" Yagoreb asked.

The short man nodded. "I never saw Limper, but I've seen many things he made. We'll set this fellow to making something. If he makes it skillfully and well, then we'll know he's Limper."

"Why should he make anything skillfully and well? If he botches the work, he'll go free."

The short man frowned. "Why set him free? If he isn't Limper, he's no use to either of us. Kill him."

Limper said, "What do you want me to make?"

The short man frowned a second time. "When I was last in Eshgorin, I saw a tree Limper made. It was made out of silver, and the leaves were fastened to the branches in such a way that when the windows were open and a wind blew in, the leaves moved in the wind. Also there were golden birds sitting on the tree's branches. They opened and shut their mouths and whistled."

"Something like that would take a long time to make, and it'd cost a lot to make, too," Limper said. "What else did you see in Eshgorin?"

"The king's sword. He showed it to me himself. The pommel was a gold dragon coiled around itself, and there were more dragons engraved on the guard and inlaid with gold, and there was writing in a strange language engraved on the blade and inlaid with gold."

Limper said, "I wrote a curse on the blade in the language of the dragons. So far it hasn't worked."

"The king won't like to hear that."

Limper shrugged.

"Can you make something like that?" Yagoreb asked.

"I can make you a sword, and it won't take all that much time and money, unless you want gold all over it, the way the king wanted it on his sword."

The short man said, "I'll ask the Council of Hwara to let us use a smithy."

Yagoreb nodded, and they turned and went away. Limper said, "Give me some more wine."

Pretty Boy gave him the jug, and he took a big gulp. Then he wiped his mouth and handed the jug back. "I think I'll get some sleep before you two decide it's time to tie me up. It's hard as hell sleeping tied up." He lay down, his cloak around him, his back to the campfire, and shut his eyes. The Geshurite woke him sometime in the middle of the night and said, "We've got to tie you up now. We're going to go to sleep."

Limper swore at him. The Geshurite grinned and tied him up, then left him to lie down and try to go back to sleep. The next day a little after sunrise, Yagoreb came back. Limper was awake, but Pretty Boy and the Geshurite weren't, and they were lying far enough away from him that it would've been hard work for him to get to them to wake them up and make them untie him. There was another man with Yagoreb. This one was dressed like a Hwaraite in a kilt and a sleeveless jacket. He was short, broad-shouldered, barrel-chested, his bare arms thick. He looked at Limper, then looked at Yagoreb. "Didn't anyone ever tell

you smiths are sacred like poets and lunatics? If
you tie one up like a chicken going to market, the
gods get angry."

Yagoreb shrugged. "These are hard times, and
no one is as pious as he ought to be."

"That may be," the man said, "but I don't intend
to allow impiety around me, if I can help it. Untie
him."

After a moment Yagoreb went over to the
Geshurite and kicked him. The Geshurite swore
and sat up. "Untie the smith," Yagoreb said.

The Geshurite got up and said, "The gods help
me in my time of pain." He went over to Limper
and untied the ropes around Limper's hands and
feet. Limper stood up, somewhat unsteadily.

The man said, "I'm Telgir Etrin, the president of
the iron-workers' society."

"Do you have somewhere for me to work?"
Limper asked.

"My own smithy," Telgir said.

"Then let's go there. I might as well start working now."

Yagoreb said to the Geshurite, "Wake Pretty Boy
and go with him. The ambassador hasn't paid me
yet."

"All right," the Geshurite said. He shook Pretty
Boy awake, and the four of them went up the hill
together and into the city, through the inner gate.
The gate had iron doors, and there were guards at
the doors. The buildings in the city were stone and
three or four stories high. The streets were paved
with stone with deep gutters on either side for
rainwater and refuse. There were men of every
kind there, some off the steppe and others out of
the mountains. The mountain men wore fur cloaks
and had tattooed faces. The steppe folk wore pants

and embroidered shirts. Their cloaks were of felt trimmed with fur, and some of them had tied brightly colored feathers on their long, dark, tangled hair. There were men, too, from the great cities of the south and east. They wore long robes and a lot of jewelry. Once Limper saw a tall, yellow-haired northerner, his face sunburned bright red. A little way from the gate, they turned into a side street. There was a tanner's shop close by. Limper could smell the dog dung used in tanning. Halfway down the street, men were taking bolts of cloth off the backs of horses. The horses filled the street from side to side, so they had to squeeze by along the wall. The smithy was at the end of the street. It was empty, the forge fires out, the bellows hung up on the wall, the tools set down on benches: hammers of different weights, tongs, chisels and shears. Limper looked around, then said, "It'll do. What about the metal?"

"Here," Telgir said and led him into a storeroom. There were bars of iron stacked on the floor, also round cakes of steel from the cities of the east. Limper looked at the cakes of steel, then said, "I'll need someone to work the bellows for me."

"I'll do that," Telgir said.

Limper looked at him. "What?"

"If one of my apprentices works with you, he'll learn new ways of doing things from you, and then he'll argue with me for months about how I should do this or that."

"All right," Limper said. "We might as well get a fire going."

Telgir nodded and went to get charcoal. While Telgir got the fire going, Limper found himself a leather apron and hefted the hammers till he found two he liked. Then he went and got a cake of the eastern steel. By this time the forge fire was burning well. Limper looked at the brightly-glowing coals and Telgir working the bellows, his face beginning to shine with sweat. He grinned, set the cake of steel in the fire and got hammer and tongs.

When the cake was hot enough to work, he began beating it. The steel wasn't the same quality throughout. On the outside of the cake, it was hard and brittle. At the center of the cake, it was soft. He had to make sure that the two kinds of metal were intermixed. He beat the piece of steel until it was long and flat. Then, he bent it over the anvil, so that it was shaped like a narrow archway. He turned this archway on its side, holding it with the tongs, and beat it flat. After that, he reheated the steel. He bent it a second time, then beat the two sides of the archway back together. When he was done, he straightened up, stretched and rubbed his hands. "I will be sore tomorrow."

Telgir grinned.

Limper heated the steel a third time. He made the archway and beat it back into a single, flat piece of steel.

Telgir nodded. "Three times through the archway, and the sword will not break. So my grandfather said."

"I do it five times," Limper answered. "Sometimes six." He kept on working. When it began to get dark, he said to Telgir, "Tell the guards where they can get lamps."

"In the storeroom in the back," Telgir said.

The guards got lamps and lit them. Limper kept working. His back and arms began to ache, and the fire's smoke began to bother his eyes.

While it was still twilight, Yagoreb came in. He stopped and watched Limper work, then said, "You seem to know what you're doing."

Limper looked up. "Shut up and get out." Then he looked back at the glowing steel.

After a moment Yagoreb left.

At last, late at night, Limper lifted the blade away from the coals and set it down, then put aside the hammer and the tongs. He stretched and rubbed his arms. "It's good steel. Do you have any wine?"

Telgir nodded. He went into one of the storerooms, then came out with a jug. He gave it to Limper, then sat down beside him. Limper drank, then handed the jug to Telgir. Telgir drank and handed it back, and Limper gave it to the Geshurite.

"Why'd you leave Eshgorin?" Telgir asked.

"I don't like working for other men," Limper said. He looked at Pretty Boy, who had the jug, and said, "Don't drink it all."

Yagoreb came back a little while later. By then Limper was lying on a bench, looking up at the ceiling. "Is he a good smith?" Yagoreb asked Telgir.

"He knows one or two things about metal working," Telgir said.

Limper turned his head and looked at Telgir, who was sitting on the floor, the empty jug in front of him. "One or two things?" he said.

"Three or four," Telgir said. "Maybe five."

Yagoreb looked at the Geshurite and Pretty Boy. "Are you drunk, too?"

Pretty Boy said, "A mouse couldn't have gotten drunk on what they let us have."

"Why should they be drunk?" Telgir said. "They

did nothing all day. We worked." He stood up. "Let's go to my house, Limper. I've more wine there."

"No," Yagoreb said.

"Why not?" Telgir asked.

"He'll be safer here, if you have a room with a good lock on the door."

Telgir frowned. He sat down at the end of the bench Limper was lying on, then looked at Limper. "Will you give your word to the merchant you won't try to get away?"

"No," Limper said.

The Geshurite said, "What are promises except words? What are words except wind? All men break wind at one time or another."

Limper sat up and looked at the Geshurite. "You must've got more wine than I thought you did." Then he said, "If you're going to lock me up, do it. I want to get some sleep."

They put him in a storeroom with bags of charcoal stacked along the walls. There was one small window with bars across it. He lay down on the floor and went to sleep. Some time later he woke. There was someone out in the street, singing about his peerless Ataia, while a companion beat on a drum and a second companion tried to play a flute. The singer sounded pretty drunk. Limper sighed and listened till the musicians had passed on down the street. Then he rolled over and went back to sleep. When he woke again in the morning, the muscles in his arms and back and chest were stiff, and it hurt him to move. There were even a couple of blisters on the palms of his hands. He shouted, "Let me out of this hole."

The Geshurite let him out. Telgir was sitting on a bench, eating a piece of cheese. "Here," he said and tossed another piece to Limper. Limper caught it. "It's goat cheese. The mountain men make it."

"What I want is water or milk, if you have it," Limper said.

There was a basket beside Telgir. He took a jug out of it, opened the jug and sniffed at it, then gave it to Limper. "Milk. My wife packed bread and sausages as well."

Limper drank half the milk, then sat down next to the basket and bit into the cheese. He looked at Pretty Boy and the Geshurite and said, his mouth full, "Is there enough for them?"

Telgir nodded. "Take what you want."

The two guards came over and took bread and sausages and began to eat.

When the food was gone, they got the forge fire going. Limper heated a new piece of steel and beat it out till it was long and narrow, then welded it onto the blade to make the tang, around which he would build the sword hilt when he got to that part of the job. At first his arms, chest and back hurt every time he lifted the hammer and every time he brought it down. The blisters on his hands broke. His head started to ache. He went through all the curses he knew, in his language and the language of Eshgorin and the language of the dragons.

A little before noon, one of Telgir's sons brought lunch: meat pies and wine. By that time the blade was finished from point to tang. Limper put it aside, and they ate. After lunch Telgir brought out a sandstone grinding wheel, and Limper began to grind the blade. He spent all afternoon doing that, swearing often, for it was slow work, and it made his back hurt. At last, late in the afternoon, he stopped and stretched and rubbed the back of his neck. Then he said, "If I hadn't had the bad luck to get myself lamed, I could've taken up an easy trade such as soldiering."

Another one of Telgir's sons brought supper in then: roast goat, bread and wine, dates and honey cakes. They sat down and ate. While they were eating Telgir said, "What do you temper steel in?"

"Whatever's at hand," Limper said. "Most of the time in Eshgorin I used either palm oil or cottonseed oil. I met a fellow once who said in his country the smiths tempered steel in honey. I tried it, and it worked well enough. I've never tried blood, though the old stories say smiths used to temper weapons in it." Limper drank some wine. "What do you use for tempering?"

Telgir frowned, then after a moment he said, "I have my own recipe that I worked out myself, and I've never told anyone about it. But I'd like to be able to say that I'd taught the master smith of Eshgorin something." He looked around to make sure that Pretty Boy and the Geshurite were nowhere near, then leaned toward Limper and said softly, "It's a mixture—the juice of radishes, cut up earthworms, and urine from a redheaded boy."

"Now that's something I've never heard of before," Limper said. "Do you have any trouble finding a redheaded boy? Most of the people I've seen here have dark hair."

Telgir nodded. "If I can't find one, I use goat piss instead."

"I see," Limper said. "Does the goat have to be any particular color?"

Telgir looked at him and frowned. "No."

"I'd like to try that recipe," Limper said. "Could you get the ingredients together tomorrow?"

Telgir nodded.

Limper finished eating, then said to the Geshurite, "Stop stuffing food into your mouth and lock me up."

He went into the storeroom, and the Geshurite locked the door after him. Then he lay down and went to sleep. He woke up in the middle of the night and heard a scratching sound. He looked up at the window. There was bright moonlight outside, and he saw Nargri squeezing in between the window's bars. She got through, jumped down onto a bag of charcoal, tumbled off the bag onto the floor, sat up and said, "There are rats out there almost as big as I am. Do you have anything to eat?"

"No," Limper said.

"Then I'm going to sleep." She curled up next to him and closed her eyes. After a while Limper went to sleep too.

When he woke in the morning Nargri was sitting on a bag of charcoal, licking one of her forefeet. For a while he did nothing except watch her. She was sitting in sunlight. Her dark grey scales shimmered the way fish scales did when the fish was newly taken from the water. Her eyes were the clear orange color of amber. When she was done licking her foot, she looked at him and said, "I'm hungry, and my feet hurt."

"And you wish you'd stayed at home with mother. How'd you find me?"

"I followed the caravan till it came to this city. That part wasn't difficult, though my feet got sore. I got through the outer gate by waiting till a wagon went through and running in underneath it. Then I hid in a gully till it was dark, and then went and found Yagoreb's camp." Nargri stopped speaking for a moment, then said, "I didn't like that part. I was afraid the scouts would kill me if they found me."

"They probably would have," Limper said.

"I saw you in the camp, Limper, but I didn't think I could get to you without somebody seeing me. So I hid in another gully. Then the next day I saw them take you into the city. I followed, but I was afraid to go through the inner gate. There were guards there with spears. So I waited till some people went through, and I went through with them. I don't think the guards saw me, but I know the people did. One of them kicked me. Then I ran and hid and when it got to be dark, I started looking for smithies. I'd heard them at Yagoreb's camp, talking about taking you to a smithy. That's all there is to tell, except that the rats in this city are enormous, and I hope you can keep yourself out of trouble after this."

"I'll do my best," Limper said. He heard a key going into the lock and said softly, "Get out of sight."

Nargri got behind a bag. The Geshurite opened the door, and Limper stood up and went out into the smithy. Telgir was nowhere in sight. Pretty Boy said, "The smith said he'd be back around noon."

Limper nodded, then ate breakfast, which was in a basket on a bench. Then he went back to grinding the blade. He finished sometime before noon, then settled himself in the smithy's doorway and drank wine. The day was bright with only a few small clouds in sight. A brisk wind blew and kept changing direction, so sometimes he smelled pine trees and sometimes the tanner's shop. Down the street he saw men loading sacks full of something onto a cart. After a while the wine and the warm sunlight made him sleepy, and he dozed off. He woke when someone poked him in the ribs. He opened his eyes. The ambassador from Eshgorin stood over him. This time he had on a blue robe and a wide belt made of elaborately worked silver plaques. "So you call this work?" the ambassador asked.

"No," Limper said.

"Well, get to work."

"Go away," Limper said and shut his eyes.

The ambassador poked him again. Limper got to his feet and went into the smithy. The ambassador followed him. Pretty Boy and the Geshurite were squatting down, playing dice. They looked up, then stood quickly. Limper picked up a hammer, then turned and said, "Get out before I use this to reshape your head."

The ambassador's face turned red. He looked at Pretty Boy and the Geshurite. "Take that hammer away from him."

They shook their heads. The Geshurite said, "We work for Yagoreb, not for you, sir, and Yagoreb wants that sword made. I don't know how Heshkya's going to make a sword unless he has a hammer."

"Get out," Limper said.

"The king will hear about this. He can deal with you as he wishes," the ambassador said and turned and left. Limper set down the hammer.

Pretty Boy said, "Did you do things like that when you worked for the king of Eshgorin?"

"Not to the king, if that's what you mean," Limper said. "I was as polite as I could be to him."

"I've heard that kings set a high value on politeness," the Geshurite said.

"This one did. I don't know about other kings."

Midway through the afternoon Telgir came back, carrying two big covered pots. He set them down, then said, "That's two of the ingredients. I've set my sons to digging up the third ingredient."

Soon after that two of Telgir's sons came in. One of them carried a covered pot, which he gave to Telgir, saying, "Here are the things you told us to get, papa."

The other boy carried a basket, which he set down, saying, "And mama sent dinner."

"We'd better eat before tempering the sword," Limper said. "I've been drinking wine all afternoon, and I like to be sober when I work."

"That sounds like a good idea to me," the Geshurite said.

Telgir nodded and waved his sons out, then took the food out of the basket. His wife had sent over a pot of beef stew and bread and wine and goat's cheese. They ate. After they'd eaten, Telgir brought a big iron pot out of one of the storerooms, then said to the guards, "You two take this out back and fill it from the well."

"That's not our job," the Geshurite said.

"It's not much to ask," Limper said, "after Telgir's fed you so much food."

"That's true," Pretty Boy said. The two of them took the pot out and brought it back full of cold water. Then Limper built the forge fire and laid the sword blade in it and heated it till it was orange in color. Then he put it into the water. The hot metal hissed loudly, and a cloud of steam came up out of the pot. When the blade had cooled, Limper took it out of the water and put it back into the forge fire to reheat. "I'm done with the water," he said. The two guards took the pot to the smithy's front door and emptied it into the street.

Then Telgir said to them, "There are two doors that lead out of here, and you two can watch them to make sure Limper doesn't run off. But I don't want you inside while I mix my recipe. It's a secret, and I want it to stay a secret."

After a moment Pretty Boy shrugged, then nodded, and he and the Geshurite went out of the smithy. Telgir shut both the smithy doors. After that he began to mix the urine, radish juice and chopped earthworms in the iron pot. While he was working he said, "I'd better tell you, I put your case before the Council of Hwara and asked them to give you asylum. They said it's impossible this far from Eshgorin to determine the truth of this matter and whether or not the king has the right to your services. For, they said, you may be a slave or a convict or an indentured servant. They say Yagoreb had broken no law here, and we are at peace with Eshgorin and, that being so, they can see no reason to take anything from either Yagoreb or the Eshgrini king."

Limper shrugged. When the sword blade was red hot, he dropped it into the mixture in the pot. Once again the metal sizzled, and steam came out. This time the steam had a horrible smell. Limper grimaced and moved away. When the blade had cooled, Limper took it out of the pot and set it down, the tongs beside it. Then he and Telgir took the pot out back and emptied it into the alley. Pretty Boy was there. Limper said, "You can come back in."

When they got back inside they found Yagoreb and the Eshgrini ambassador there. This time the ambassador had on a brown robe with long panels of red and yellow embroidery sewn on it in front. Yagoreb said, "I'm planning to leave Hwara in two days, and I want this matter settled one way or the other before then."

Limper looked at Telgir. "Do you find when you make things for people, they won't leave you alone?"

Telgir nodded. "I tell them good work takes time; I tell them I do worse work when I'm interrupted ten times a day; but they still come and buzz like flies all about me."

"These fellows are pretty bad that way," Limper said. "But the king of Eshgorin was worse."

"When will the sword be done?" Yagoreb asked.

"Another day, if you leave me alone to work on it," Limper said. "Come back the day after tomorrow in the morning."

"All right," Yagoreb said, and he and the ambassador left.

After they were gone Pretty Boy said, "I don't think I'd like to be inside your skin when you get back to Eshgorin, and the king reads the report that that ambassador is going to write on you."

Limper picked up a wine jug and shook it, then took a swallow of wine. "I've been working long enough so I know which people it's safe to be rude to. If that fellow were somebody the king listened to, he'd be in Eshgorin or in one of the great capitals, such as Anyar or Essim." He picked up a piece of cheese and the heel of a loaf of bread left over from dinner, then walked into the storeroom, sat down on the floor and called, "All right. Lock me up."

Pretty Boy shut the door and locked it. Nargri came out from behind a bag of charcoal, and Limper gave her the bread and cheese. He drank wine while she ate. When she was done she said, "Do you plan to go back to Eshgorin?"

"No."

"Then what do you plan to do?"

"Get out of here."

"How?" Nargri asked.

After a moment Limper said, "What we did last time worked until Norem Archer used his bow."

"You want me to bite somebody."

Limper nodded.

"Who?"

"Pretty Boy or the Geshurite."

"I'll bite the Geshurite," Nargri said. "Pretty Boy looks as if he might have a greasy taste."

"I'll work late tomorrow. After dark you come out and get as close to the Geshurite as you can. When I go after Pretty Boy, you go after the Geshurite."

"What about the third fellow? Who goes after him?"

"It isn't his quarrel," Limper said. "He'll stay out of it."

"So you say," Nargri said. "It isn't much of a plan."

"The best plans are simple."

"This one seems simple-minded."

"I'm going to sleep," Limper said, and lay down.

He woke the next morning and heard somebody opening the door. He sat up and looked around. Nargri was out of sight. The Geshurite came in. He had a piece of cheese. He said, "Telgir is here, and he's brought breakfast with him." He bit into the cheese, then said, his mouth full, "They make cheese like this in Geshur."

Limper went out and greeted Telgir, got a piece of cheese, then went to the door. The sky was bright and cloudless. The air was cold. Looking west, he could see the mountains. There was snow on the high peaks. "How long before snow closes the passes?" he asked.

"A month," Telgir said. "Maybe more. Maybe less."

Limper nodded and went back to look at the food Telgir had brought. There was a bowl full of a soft, white, sour-smelling stuff. "What's that?"

"Curdled goat's milk," the Geshurite said. "Try it."

"They make that in Geshur, too?" Limper asked.

"Yes. My mother made the best in town. She probably still does, unless she's dead."

Limper looked at Pretty Boy. "Where do you come from? You've never told me."

"Eshgorin," Pretty Boy said. "The part of the city they call the Rat's Hole."

"Is that so?" Limper said. Then he said to Telgir, "I need some wood—good, close-grained hardwood—and the tools to work it. Also some cord. Red silk cord, if you can get it."

"I'll have to go out," Telgir said.

Limper nodded, went into the storeroom where the iron and steel were kept and got a bar of iron. When he came back Telgir was gone. Limper got the forge fire going and heated the iron and made the sword's upper and lower guards. Telgir came back early in the afternoon, bringing a piece of cherry wood, wood-working tools, and lunch. By that time Limper was done making the guards. They ate, then Limper sawed off a long narrow piece of wood and carved away its corners till it was a cylinder. Then he bored through the cylinder's center, so a hole went through it lengthwise. This took him most of the afternoon, and he cut himself a couple of times with the tools he used. "I've never been as good with wood as with metal," he said after he'd cut himself the second time. Finally he set the cylinder aside and rebuilt the fire. When the fire was burning well, he fitted the sword's lower guard onto the tang so it rested on the sword's shoulders. Then he heated the tang, then fitted the wooden cylinder onto it. The hole through the cylinder was a little too narrow for the tang, and he had to force the cylinder on while the hot metal burnt the wood and made the hole bigger. When the cylinder was all the way on, he put the upper guard onto the tang on top of it, then bent over the part of the tang that came out through the guard and riveted it to the guard. Lastly he wound the red silk cord around the cylinder till the wood was completely hidden. He knotted the cord tightly, then laid the sword down on the floor and looked at it. He said, "I don't think the ambassador will like it. There's no gold on it anywhere. He seems to me to be the kind of man who thinks that if a thing glitters, it must be well-made."

"If you want me to, I'll tell him in my opinion it's pretty well-made," Telgir said.

"Thanks," Limper said. After that he ate supper standing in the smithy's open door. It was after sunset. The evening star was out, and a half moon. The air was cold and still. After supper he took a file and filed smooth the rough spots on the guards. When he stopped and the smithy was silent, he heard a skittering sound. Pretty Boy said, "What's that?" and stood up and looked around.

"There;" Telgir said and pointed to a corner.

"That lizard of yours," Pretty Boy said. "It followed you."

"So she did."

Nargri came out of the shadow into the light and

blinked her eyes, then went over to where the Geshurite was sitting, half drunk and half asleep. "Call it off," the Geshurite said. "I don't like scaly things."

Nargri leaped up onto the bench beside him and bit his right forearm. The Geshurite yelled. Pretty Boy started to pull his sword out of its scabbard. Limper grabbed up his sword and brought it down onto Pretty Boy's shoulder. He hadn't sharpened its edges yet. It broke the skin, but it didn't cut deep. Still Pretty Boy let go of his sword. He grabbed his shoulder, his face going white.

Limper looked to the Geshurite, who was standing up and holding his arm, which was bleeding. Then he looked to Telgir and said, "What do you intend to do?"

"Nothing," Telgir said. "If I fight you, one of us might be killed, and there are too few good smiths as it is."

"Then all three of you throw your swords on the floor and get in there," Limper said and pointed to the storeroom where he'd been kept.

Pretty Boy and the Geshurite looked at one another. The Geshurite shrugged and said, "This is only a job." He drew his sword and tossed it onto the floor, then went into the storeroom. Pretty Boy followed him. Telgir had no weapon except a small knife, which he threw down. Then he followed Pretty Boy. Limper said, "I'll be here for a while, working on the sword. If any one of you makes a sound, I'll kill all of you."

"You might find that difficult," Pretty Boy said.

"Do you intend to find out whether or not I can do it?" Limper asked.

"No."

Limper locked the door, then said to Nargri, "Stay by the door. If you hear anything, tell me."

"Can't you finish the sword later?"

"Do as I say," Limper said. Then he ground edges onto the sword blade. When he was done he looked around the smithy, picked up a coil of rope, a bridle with an iron bit and bronze mountings, a roll of gold wire, two jars of wine, and a large rag.

"Are you taking the whole smithy with you?" Nargri.

"Only what I think I can use."

She watched him wrap the rag around his sword until it was hard to tell what the sword was, then she said, "There are two scabbards in there." She pointed at the storeroom door.

"And three men as well, and chances are none of them is feeling friendly toward me. I'm not going in there unless I have to." There was still some of the red silk cord left. Limper used it to tie the two wine jugs together. Then he took the gold wire and put it inside his shirt. "Come on," he said. They went outside together, Limper loaded down with the wine jugs, the rope, the sword and the bridle. Most of the buildings along the street were dark. Here and there light shone out of a second or third story window. The moon was still up. A street or two away men were playing flutes and singing.

"Do you know the way to the wall?" Limper asked.

"Follow me." Nargri went past a couple of buildings, then into an alley, Limper behind her. The alley was narrow, so narrow in some spots that he had to turn sideways to get through. The air stank, and the ground was soft and slippery underfoot. He realized that there must be windows opening onto the alley out of which people threw refuse. He couldn't see Nargri. It was too dark. He followed the sound she made. She moved quickly. With his bad leg and the load he carried, he had trouble keeping up with her. Twice they came out into a street and crossed it, going into another narrow, foul-smelling alley. When they came out of the third alley they were opposite the wall. Nargri stopped and said, "What now?"

The wall was forty feet tall, give or take a foot or two, and it was built out of big blocks of stone. The blocks were so carefully fitted together that he could barely make out the lines where they met, though bright moonlight lit the wall.

"There must be stairs somewhere going to the top."

"So you say," Nargri said. "Which way do we go?"

"Away from the gate."

"All right." Nargri turned up the street, and Limper followed her. They passed four or five side streets. Then they came to where a flight of stairs went up the wall. "I suppose," Nargri said, "you want me to go up and look around."

"Yes."

"My mother's going to have a few words to say to you, when she finds out how you've been taking care of me."

"More than a few words, but I'll worry about that later."

Nargri went up the stairs. Limper waited for her in the street. After a while she came back and said, "No one in sight."

He went up the stairs, Nargri a couple of steps ahead of him. At the top of the stairs there was a guardwalk along the wall a little below the battlemented parapet. He looked out through one of the deep notches in the wall's top and saw fires where a caravan was camped. Beyond the fires he saw the outer wall, and, beyond that, the mountains. He set down his sword and the wine jugs and the bridle. Then he uncoiled the rope and made one end fast around one of the tall blocks of stone that jutted up between the notches.

Nargri said, "Someone is coming."

Limper turned and looked. There was a man coming along the guardwalk toward him. The moon was still high enough so he could see the fellow pretty clearly. He wore a helmet and a mail shirt, and he carried a spear. Limper looked around and saw nowhere to hide. It wasn't likely that he could outrun the man. He picked up his sword and waited. The soldier came closer, stopped and said, "What're you doing here?"

"I came up to piss."

"What's wrong with the street?" the soldier asked. "And what's the rope for?"

"I was planning to hang myself afterward. I didn't want to get my pants wet when I did it."

"I think I'd better take you to see my captain."

"Can I take my belongings with me? I was planning to leave them for whoever came along, since I couldn't figure out how to take them with me into the afterlife. But if I'm not going to die, I'll need them."

After a moment the soldier said, "All right." By this time he was close enough to Limper to stick his spear into him. Limper bent, then straightened up quickly. He grabbed the spear shaft with his free hand, stepped forward and jabbed the rag-wrapped sword into the soldier's gut. The soldier grunted and bent double. Limper dropped the sword and yanked the spear away from him, then shoved the spear butt into his neck. The soldier stumbled backward. By this time he was having trouble staying on his feet. Limper turned the spear around and said, "Keep quiet."

The soldier had his arms wrapped around his midsection, and he was retching.

"That isn't what I'd call quiet," Nargri said.

The man was bent almost double. Limper brought the spear shaft down across the back of his neck. The man fell forward onto the pavement and lay still. Limper tossed down the spear, saying to Nargri, "Watch him. If he starts stirring, tell me."

"All right," Nargri said.

Limper tugged at the rope to make sure it was securely fastened to the block of stone, then tossed the free end of the rope over the wall. Then he went to the soldier and rolled him over onto his back, unbuckled his sword belt and tugged it out from under him. He buckled the belt on. "I ought to kill him. If there are any gods listening who care about human life, remember I didn't stick a sword into this fellow. You can reward me by letting me get out of here." While he spoke he unwrapped his sword, then pulled the soldier's sword from its scabbard, tossed it down and put his sword into the scabbard. The scabbard was a little too short and too wide, so he tore off a piece of the rag he'd wrapped around his sword and wedged it into the scabbard to hold his sword in place.

The soldier groaned and stirred. Limper swore and tore the rag into two pieces. He used one to tie the soldier's hands behind his back and the other to gag him. Then he pulled the soldier's kilt down around his ankles and used it to tie his legs together. After that Limper picked up Nargri and set her on top of the parapet, then picked up the bridle and the wine jugs and hung them around his neck. "As soon as I'm down, you follow me," he said to Nargri. "And watch the soldier meanwhile." He pulled himself up onto the parapet, got hold of the rope and went down it hand over hand. It wasn't easy to do. His arms were still sore from the work in the smithy, and the wine jugs kept bumping against his chest. The cord they hung on cut into the back of his neck. He could hear the soft jingle of the bridle's bit, along with the harsh sound his breath made. When he got to the end of the rope he was still several feet from the ground. "Why do these things happen to me?" he asked. He hung at the rope's end for a moment or two, then let go and dropped the rest of the way. When he hit the ground he stumbled and fell. He swore, then felt the wine jugs to make sure they were unbroken. After that he stood up. Above him Nargri said, "There isn't any more rope, Limper."

He looked up. He could barely see her, a black spot swinging back and forth overhead. "Drop. I'll catch you."

"All right," she said and dropped. She landed across his right shoulder, started to slide off and dug in her claws.

"Let go," he said loudly and grabbed her. She pulled out her claws. He set her down and rubbed his shoulder. "It's lucky for you I promised your mother that I'd see you came to no harm." He took the piece of cloth out of the scabbard so he could pull out his sword if he had to, then started away from the wall. Nargri followed him.

The ground sloped down slightly. It had been grazed bare by caravan animals, and there were shallow gullies every ten or twenty feet, dry at this time of year. A couple of times he almost stepped into a gully before he saw it and stopped. Ahead of him and to his left he saw campfires, men lying close by them, amid piles of trade goods. He went to the right, making a wide circle around the campfires, moving as quickly as he was able. The wind changed, and a horse whinnied. A man standing by one of the piles of trade goods turned and looked around. Limper stopped and stood still till the man turned away, then he went on. The gate was ahead of him, lit by torches, two soldiers standing in front of it, leaning on their spears. The doors were twice as tall as a man, made of wood bound with iron, with a thick, iron-bound bar across them, keeping them shut.

Nargri said softly, "It seems to me it would've been a better idea to escape during the day. The gates are open then."

"You may be right," Limper said. "Well, we're going to have to get through somehow. I shouldn't take the time to get a horse, but I'm going to. I don't like being on foot when I'm being chased. You stay here." He set the wine jugs down and went back to where he'd seen horses tethered, a short distance from one of the groups of campfires. When he got close he stopped and looked till he saw the man guarding them. He was sitting on a bale of hay, his spear leaning against the bale. He'd taken his helmet off. He was scratching his head and doing a thorough job of it. Limper circled till the horses were between him and the guard, then walked up to the horses, going slowly so he didn't startle them. They turned their heads to look at him, and a couple of them moved uneasily. Limper said softly and gently, "There's nothing to worry about. Don't give me away." He picked out a horse and let it get a good look at him, so it knew he wasn't anything a horse might be afraid of, then he squatted down and untied its tether. When he stood up the horse snorted and jerked its head back. Limper said softly, "I'm not going to hurt you, you idiot." After that he led the horse away from the other horses. When he got a short distance from the herd, he stopped and looked back at the man guarding the horses. He'd finished scratching his head by this time. Now he had his head tilted back, and he was scratching his beard with both hands. Limper grinned and led the horse on.

He stopped a little way from Nargri, upwind so the smell of Nargri wouldn't startle the horse, then put the bridle he'd brought along on the horse. After that he tied the horse to a bare-branched bush. "Now keep quiet," he said to it. He went back to where Nargri was and said, "Get as close as you can to the soldiers without them seeing you. When I'm close enough to them to go after one of them, you come in after the other."

"I'm getting pretty tired of biting people," Nargri said.

Limper picked up the wine jugs and slung them over one shoulder, then went back and got the horse, leading it toward the gate. When he was close enough so the torches lit him, the soldiers straightened up and got better grips on their spears. One of them called, "Who's there?"

Limper stopped and said, "My name's Heshkya, if that tells you anything. Does either one of you want to buy a horse?"

The soldier who'd spoken before said, "That's not much of a horse."

Limper unplugged one of the wine jugs and

drank out of it. Then he looked the horse over.
"I've seen better, but I've seen worse, too."

"What happened to your saddle?" the second
soldier asked.

"I won this fellow in a dice game. Somebody
else won the saddle. I thought if I sold the horse,
I'd have enough money for a night on the town.
The first day out of here, everybody's going to be
stumbling along, moaning and groaning and saying
what a wonderful time he'd had in Hwara. I don't
want to have to lie about it." He took another
drink.

The first soldier said, "If you aren't going to
share that, go away. I'm not going to stand here
and watch you drink while my tongue shrivels in
my mouth."

Limper came closer, leading the horse, and
swung the jugs down onto the ground. He untied
them and gave one jug to one of the soldiers, keeping the other jug for himself. The soldiers drank.
Then the first soldier said, "You came in with one
of the caravans?"

Limper nodded. "And I'll go out with it, unless I
can find another job, which doesn't seem likely."

The first soldier shook his head. "There's no
work here these days."

The second soldier, who had the wine jug and
was drinking out of it, looked to one side. "What in
hell is that?" Wine spilled out of the jug onto the
soldier's shirt. He swore and looked down. Limper
glanced over and saw Nargri running toward them,
then swung the jug he held into the first soldier's
face. The jug broke. The soldier stumbled back.
Limper turned, starting to pull out his sword. The
second soldier had dropped the jug and got ahold

of his spear. He was holding it so it was pointing at Limper's gut. Limper stepped back, lifting his hand away from his sword hilt. "I surrender."

Nargri got to the soldier. She jumped onto the soldier's leg and dug in her claws. The soldier yelled, let go of his spear and grabbed at Nargri with both hands. She bit one hand, and he yelled again. Limper pulled out his sword. "Shut up or I'll kill you." He saw something moving to one side and looked toward it. It was the first soldier, stumbling toward him. His face was covered with wine and blood. He had dropped his spear, and he was trying to get his sword out of its scabbard. Limper said, "Stop that." The soldier stopped and stood still. Limper looked at the second soldier. He was beating at Nargri with one hand and trying to pull out his sword with the other hand.

Limper said, "Let go of that sword, and the two of you get the gate open."

The second soldier let go of his sword hilt. "Get this thing off me."

"Off him, Nargri."

Nargri dropped onto the ground. The soldier turned and kicked her. She tumbled over, then got up and said in the language of the dragons, "Kill him, Limper."

Limper said to the soldiers, "Open the gate."

They looked at one another, and then shrugged. The second soldier said, "I think we'll have to do it, but the captain isn't going to be happy with us." They slid the bar back and pulled the door open.

Someone up on the wall yelled, "What's going on down there?"

Limper got up onto the horse as fast as he could, then leaned down and grabbed up Nargri and kicked the horse. It started toward the gate. One of the soldiers started to shut the door he held, then looked at Limper coming toward him and ran off, shouting. The other soldier jumped back out of the way. Limper went past him through the gate. Now he rode between stone walls, his head bent low so he wouldn't hit the gate ceiling. He heard shouts behind him. He felt Nargri digging her claws into his pants, scratching his legs. Limper kicked the horse again. It lengthened its stride, carrying him out of the gate. There were no torches there. In a moment or two he was in the dark. Behind him on the wall an alarm horn bellowed.

A short way beyond the gate he slowed the horse. Alarm horns still sounded on the wall but, as far as he could tell, no one was following him. "Do you hear anyone coming?" he asked Nargri.

"No."

The night was moonless by this time, and so dark that it was hard for him to see the road. He kept the horse to a walk. When dawn came he turned the horse off the road into the hills, going north. Nargri had been sleeping while he held onto her. She woke up and said, "I'm hungry."

"I knew I'd forgotten something," Limper said. "I didn't bring any food."

IN THE MOUNTAINS

They rode north from Hwara through the foothills, the high mountains to their left. The hilltops were forested. In the valleys were yellow fields of wheat and mustard, and pastures where goats and cattle grazed. Limper kept to the high slopes in the shelter of the trees. From time to time he stopped and looked at the road below him, watching for the flash of sunlight on armor. As far as he could tell, no one was following them. About midday Nargri started complaining that she was hungry.

"You'll have to wait," Limper said. "I'm not going down there to ask for food." He waved at the farm below them. The house was in between the road and a small river that sparkled in the sunlight. The air was still enough so they could hear the farm dog barking.

"Why not?" Nargri asked. "You worry too much, Limper. No one is going to chase you this far."

Limper shrugged, then nudged his horse. It went on, following a narrow trail between the pines.

Nargri kept complaining about hunger. Finally Limper said, "If you mention hunger one more time, I'll eat you."

"It seems to me that you promised my mother you'd see I came to no harm."

"Few men expect to keep all the promises they make."

"Is that so?"

Limper nodded.

At sundown they came to some broken walls high on a hill. There was a tall stone pillar there, the only thing still standing. Limper reined his horse and looked around. There were no signs of people. He dismounted, then lifted Nargri down.

"That's dragon work," she said. "We used to build signal fires on top of pillars long, long ago."

"Are you sure?"

Nargri nodded.

"With any luck, the people around here are still afraid of it."

"Why should they be? They don't even believe in dragons."

"No, but they might remember that something about this place is bad."

"Oh."

There was a stream close by. Limper led the horse to it to drink, then tethered the horse in a clearing full of grass. By this time it was twilight. He gathered branches and built a small fire where the ruin's walls would hide it. "I'm going to see if I can find some food," he said.

"Take care," Nargri said. She sounded worried.

Limper grinned, then turned and went down the

hill. The sky was dark, and the first stars were starting to appear. He went through the pine woods, then through fields of dry grass till he reached an orchard. He could make out one or two round shapes at the ends of branches. The air was full of the smell of apples. He took off his shirt and laid it on the ground, then started picking apples and putting them on the shirt. It was slow work in the darkness. After he'd gathered half a dozen apples, a dog started to bark somewhere close by. He picked up the shirt and started up the hill. At first he went as quickly as he could. But the dog didn't follow, and he went more slowly. When he reached the ruin, he found Nargri sleeping. She woke and raised her head. "What did you get?"

"Apples." He put the shirt down and unfolded it. There were five apples, all ripe and glossy red. Two of them were spotted with wormholes.

"Is that all? Couldn't you get something from the farmhouse?"

Limper shook his head. "I'm not the bravest fellow you're ever going to meet, Nargri. They had a dog down there." He sat down and picked out an apple without wormholes. "Tomorrow morning I'll see if there are any fish in that stream. When I was a lot younger, I learned how to catch fish with my bare hands. I wanted to be able to do something the other boys couldn't do."

Nargri sniffed, then started to eat an apple.

Soon after that Limper put on his shirt and lay down beside the fire to sleep. Nargri curled up beside him, so his body warmed hers.

They both woke early. The fire was out, and the morning air was cold. Limper rebuilt the fire, then went and caught two fish. He cleaned them and cooked them. After breakfast he kicked dirt over the fire, got the horse and mounted.

They kept going northward along the hilltops. The second night they slept in a shepherd's hut. It looked as if it had been empty for a long time. There was a very old piece of cheese stuck under the eaves. Limper found it by following the smell. They ate the cheese in spite of its aroma, and drank water.

"Another day like this, and I'll be sick," Nargri said.

Limper nodded. "So will I."

The next day they left the forest and went down onto the road. The valleys were narrower now. The hills were steeper and more thickly forested. There were fewer farms. On the evening of the third day they came to a house built into the side of a hill so it was half underground. Limper stopped some distance from the house and looked it over. There was a leanto off to one side and an apple orchard beyond the leanto. On the hill behind the house three goats grazed. "It ought to be safe to spend the night there. We're a long way from Hwara, and no one is following us."

"All I know is that I'm cold and hungry," Nargri said.

"Well, so am I." He rode up to the house, dismounted and knocked on the door.

"What do you want?" a woman asked.

"Supper and someplace to sleep."

The woman opened the shutters of the window beside the door and looked out. She was somewhere between 35 and 40, light-skinned and dark-haired, a little fat, but still good looking. She stared at Limper, and he noticed that her eyes were pale green. "Well, you look harmless enough." She opened the door, and he came in, Nargri following.

There were six children in the room, sitting at the table, eating supper. One of them, a boy thirteen or fourteen years old, looked at Limper, then said to the woman, "You're going to make us the talk of the neighborhood, asking men to stay here overnight."

"It's easy to see whose family you take after, Thib," the woman said. "My kin were never meanminded. Now, go out and take care of this fellow's horse."

The boy got up and went out. The woman looked at Limper. "Sit down. I'll get you something to eat." Then she looked down at Nargri. "What's that?"

"A dragon." Limper sat down at the table.

"So that's what they look like," the woman said. She brought him a piece of bread, a piece of cheese and a cup of milk. Limper broke the cheese in two and gave half to Nargri.

After a while the boy Thib came back in. He took an apple out of a bowl on the table and ate it, watching Limper. Limper finished eating and stretched out his legs, so his feet were close to the fire in the firepit. Nargri curled up beside him, still nibbling on a piece of bread. Two of the children, small boys, were playing with swords made out of branches. The smaller one said, "It's my turn to be Enrin Silvershield."

The bigger boy said, "If I'm not Enrin, I won't play."

"All right," the smaller boy said. "But next time, I get to be Enrin."

"What are they playing?"

"There was a man from the south here. He told

us stories about Enrin Silvershield, the King of Eshgorin's champion. Ever since, they've been pretending to be Enrin."

Limper grinned, then said to the bigger boy, "Come here."

The boy came over.

"I'd like to look at your sword."

The boy gave it to him. Limper turned it over. The long branch was crooked, and the short branch was splintered at both ends. The two branches were tied together with wool yarn. "If you're Enrin, then this must be the sword Lionstooth."

The boy nodded. "The man said a famous smith made it. It has a lion's head made out of gold at the end of the hilt."

Limper shook his head. "The pommel is disk shaped, and on either side there's a lion's head inlaid with gold."

"Is there a picture of the lion on the blade?" the boy asked. "The southerner said there was."

Limper nodded. "On one side. It's inlaid with gold. On the other side, there's the smith's name inlaid with iron." He gave the sword back to the boy.

"Where'd you learn so much about the sword?" the boy asked.

"I've been in Eshgorin. Everyone there can tell you all about Enrin."

"Did you ever see him?" the smaller boy asked.

Limper nodded.

The bigger boy said, "The man said Enrin was the tallest man he'd ever seen."

"Enrin's pretty tall," Limper said.

"And he has a shield made out of solid silver, made by the same smith who made his sword."

Limper shook his head. "No one makes armor

out of silver. It's too expensive and too soft. The shield is covered with silver leaf."

"You seem to be well informed about Enrin's armor," the woman said.

"That's true enough," Limper said.

Soon after the woman told the children, "Get to bed, all of you."

The children climbed up into the loft. The woman said to Limper, "You can sleep down here," and opened the doors of the sleeping cabinet.

"I don't want to take your bed away from you."

"My husband built it so it'd be big enough for two," the woman said.

"He won't mind finding me in his bed?"

"It's a long way from where he is to here," the woman said. "And it doesn't seem likely to me that he'll be coming back, for the Old Woman has him in her house. If I were you, I wouldn't worry about meeting him." She lay down inside the cabinet.

Nargri looked up at Limper, then closed her eyes and put her tail over her nose. Limper went over to the cabinet and lay down beside the woman. For a while he did nothing. Then he reached over and touched the woman's breast. She rolled over and grabbed hold of him. "I was beginning to think you weren't going to do anything."

Just then the door rattled. Limper started and looked out of the sleeping cabinet. The door was still shut. There was no one in the room except Nargri, asleep on the bench, her dark scales gleaming in the firelight.

"That was only the wind," the woman said.

"Where exactly is your husband?"

"In the Old Woman's House, in the house of the dead."

"Oh."

"He died two years ago. But I haven't forgotten what it's like to lie with a man." As she spoke, she started to undo his belt.

Limper glanced at Nargri to make sure she was asleep. Then he unbuckled his belt, took off his pants and made love with the woman, gently and a little clumsily, since he was out of practice. It was several months since he'd lain with a woman. When they were done, the woman kissed him. "Well, that wasn't bad, though my dear husband could do better. Still, better a live sparrow than a dead eagle. Good night." She rolled over and went to sleep. Limper lay awake for a while, staring out of the cabinet at the dimly glowing fire. At last he fell asleep.

The next morning he slept late. When he got up to go out and piss, Nargri got between him and the door. He squatted down and asked, "What is it?"

Nargri said in the language of the dragons, "I think you'd better be careful going outside. That boy Thib went out a while ago, and he took an ax with him. But I haven't heard him chopping wood."

Limper stood up, went back to the cabinet and buckled on his sword belt. The woman was setting food on the table. She watched him, then asked, "What're you doing that for?"

"You can't tell what you're going to meet up with," Limper said.

The door was half open. As he went out, he pushed against the door till it wouldn't open any further. Something was between it and the house wall. Limper pulled out his sword, then pulled the door away from the wall. The boy Thib was against the wall, an ax in his hand.

"You'll be a lot better off, if you put that ax down," Limper said.

"No," the boy said and leaped at him. Limper grabbed the boy's right wrist with his left hand, so he couldn't use the ax. The boy hit him in the face with his free hand. He chopped at the boy's leg with his sword, and the boy screamed.

"What is it?" the woman called.

Limper twisted the boy's wrist, and the boy dropped the ax. By this time the boy's face was white. Limper pushed him back against the wall. There was blood running down his leg from a cut in the side of his thigh.

The door opened. The woman came out, a knife in her hand. Limper moved back several steps. "Why don't you put that down? I haven't killed him, and I don't intend to."

"What happened?" the woman asked. She still held onto the knife.

"Thib decided to test his ax's edge on something other than wood."

"That was foolish of him," the woman said. She looked at the boy, who was leaning against the wall, his eyes shut. "We'd better get him inside."

They each took one of the boy's arms and half carried him inside and had him lie down in the sleeping cabinet.

"If you don't need me," Limper said, "I'm going out to piss. I didn't get around to it before."

He went out. When he came back in, the woman was putting a bandage around the boy's leg. The boy who'd pretended to be Enrin the night before was watching her. He looked at Limper and said, "I wish I were Enrin Silvershield. I'd be able to do something about you then."

"I've had days when I've wished I were Enrin,"

Limper said. "But if you're going to make wishes, there are a lot better things to wish for." Then he asked the woman, "Will he be all right?"

"How can I tell? I'm not a prophetess."

He stood watching her work for a short while longer. Then he said, "I'd better be going."

"Go, then," the woman said.

Limper took cheese and bread from the table, then went out, Nargri following him. He found his horse in the leanto beside the house, in between a cow and two nanny-goats. There was a saddle hanging there, old and battered looking. But the cinch straps and stirrup straps looked as if they'd probably hold, and he was tired of riding bareback. He took the saddle and put it on his horse, then put on his bridle and led the horse outside. Once out of the leanto, he stopped and scratched his head, then tethered the horse and went back to the house.

The woman was sitting at the table, her head in her hands. Limper cleared his throat. She looked up. "Do you have a cloak I could buy? I'm going up into the mountains, and it's going to be cold."

She sighed, then nodded and went to a chest, opening it and pulling out a fine, thick wool cloak. "Here." She held it out to him.

Limper got out the gold wire he'd taken from Telgir Etrin's smithy and laid it on the table. "I'm sorry. I meant no harm."

"Take the cloak and go," the woman said.

Limper nodded, took the cloak and went outside. He untied the horse and mounted him, then leaned down and picked up Nargri. After that they rode on.

After they'd been traveling a while Nargri said, "Why did Thib try to kill you?"

"Most likely, because I spent the night with his mother."

"If she didn't mind, why should he?"

After a moment Limper said, "If you can ask a question like that, you have a lot to learn about people."

He kept going north. The land rose into higher and higher hills. The road he followed wound through narrow valleys, full of trees, fast-running streams in the valley bottoms. Every few hundred feet little streams, no more than trickles this time of year, came down the hillside across the road. After a while the road got to the mountains and wound up between bare cliffs. That night they made camp in a high valley at the center of which was a lake surrounded by bushes. Limper waded into the lake and caught two fish, then came out and built a fire, cleaned the fish and cooked them on hot coals he raked out of the fire. They were high enough up so they could see long distances. South of them were hills covered with forest. To the west were more mountains, higher than the ones ahead of them. The sky was clear except for a few clouds in the east. "This looks like good country for dragons," Limper said.

"It used to be," Nargri said. "But all the stone doors I've seen look as if they've been shut a long time. I've been watching the high slopes, looking for signs of dragon gardens, but I haven't seen any."

The night was cold. Limper woke up several times and put more branches on the fire. In the morning the sky was grey, and the air felt damp. "We'd better hurry, if we're going to get through the passes," Limper said. They had bread and cheese for breakfast.

The road went higher into the mountains. The air grew colder. A wind started to blow. Nargri, who was crouched in front of Limper, pressed close to him to stay warm. He covered her with his cloak. The road went into a gorge, alongside a river. In some places most of the road had crumbled into the river. In other places rock-slides covered most of the road. Several times Limper dismounted and led the horse over jumbled stones or along a narrow ledge, carrying Nargri in his arms. About noon it began to snow: big flakes that melted as soon as they touched the ground. After a while the snowflakes weren't melting and the ground was turning white. Snow caught in the horse's mane and in the hair on the horse's neck. Limper kept changing the reins from hand to hand, warming the hand he wasn't using in his armpit. Nargri pressed closer to him. He touched her. She felt cold. "We'd better find shelter before my hands fall off," he said.

Sometime later he found a break in the gorge wall, a ravine going back, one side sheltered by an overhang. He dismounted and led the horse in under the overhang, then put Nargri down.

She said, "I've never been this cold before."

There were bushes growing in the ravine, bare this time of year except for a few dry leaves. Limper broke branches off them and got a fire going, and Nargri moved close to it to warm herself, so close that he said, "Be careful. You aren't a salamander."

"Salamanders live in water, not fire," Nargri said.

"Thank you for telling me." Limper went to get more firewood.

They spent the night there. Limper woke up

several times to put wood on the fire. Once he went out and gathered more wood. The snow was knee-deep by this time, but no more of it was falling. The air was still and cold. Looking up, he saw stars in between the clouds.

In the morning they ate the rest of the bread and cheese. Then they went on, Limper going on ahead of the horse to make a way through the snow. He held Nargri in his arms to keep her warm. The sky was cloudless, and the glare off the snow was so bright he had trouble seeing. He went slowly, keeping close to the gorge wall, testing the ground ahead of him before he put his full weight on it. About noon they came out of the gorge into a valley, ringed by high peaks. On the western side of the valley there was a huge mountain, higher than all the rest, the lower slopes white with snow, the high cliffs bare and black. Ahead of them on the other side of the valley, a line of smoke went straight up through the still air.

"It looks as if we might get supper after all," Limper said.

"Good," Nargri said.

The snow had drifted, and in some places the drifts were six or seven feet high; in other places the bare ground showed. They went slowly. By the time they reached the middle of the valley, it was midafternoon, and the sky was grey again. By the time they reached the far side of the valley, it was after sunset. Snow was falling. The flakes were large and wet and came down slowly. The valley narrowed. A few stunted pines grew in the shelter of the stone walls. The branches were weighted down with snow. Ahead Limper saw a gleam of light. He kept going, though his feet felt numb, and he stumbled often. Nargri, who was in his arms, kept making soft whining sounds. At length they reached a cabin built of logs. Snow covered the roof, and a huge snowdrift hid one of the side walls. All along the eaves there were icicles, some of them two feet long. The light Limper had seen came through a broken shutter on the window beside the door. Limper knocked on the door. After a moment a man opened it. He was a head taller than Limper, gaunt and grey haired, his hands huge. He looked Limper over. "There's a barn out back. Put your horse there."

Limper nodded, then led his horse to the barn. There were five horses there already. Four of them were ordinary riding horses, but one was a little yellow pony with a dark mane and tail.

"That's strange," Limper said.

"What?" Nargri asked.

"Why would a farmer have a pony?"

"Who can say? Get me into the cabin, Limper. I think I'm freezing to death."

He put his horse in the one empty stall and gave it hay and water, then went into the cabin, carrying Nargri. The man was at the firepit, bent over an iron pot, stirring the stew in it. He looked around, then straightened up. "What have you got there?"

"What does it look like?" Limper said.

"A big lizard."

"That's what it is."

"That seems to me to be a strange thing to carry around." He paused, then said, "I am Gatix."

"My name is Heshkya Atthal," Limper said.

"Sit down," Gatix said. He got a bowl and ladled some of the stew into it, then gave the bowl to Limper. Limper put Nargri down on a bench and sat down beside her. He shared the stew with her.

Gatix ladled out stew for himself and ate it, then

refilled his bowl and ate that, then refilled the bowl a third time.

"Cold weather makes you hungry," Limper said.

"Get yourself more," Gatix said. "There's plenty."

Limper refilled his bowl.

When they were done eating, Limper and Nargri got closer to the fire. Limper was getting sleepy. Nargri was soon asleep.

"I have wine," Gatix said. "Do you want some?" Limper nodded. Gatix got two cups and filled them from a jug, giving one cup to Limper. The wine was sweet and heavy, like the wine from the hill-towns northeast of Eshgorin. The wind shrieked outside the cabin. Gatix said, "That sound is the voices of the dead people, that the wind carries down from the Old Woman's House on the mountain."

"I thought the wind made that sound by itself," Limper said.

Gatix shook his head. "It's plain you don't know where you are."

"That's true enough." He was having trouble keeping his eyes open. The fire in front of him kept getting blurry. From time to time he blinked. Then, for several moments, he could see clearly.

Gatix gulped the rest of his wine. "That big mountain west of the valley is the Old Woman's Mountain."

"Is that so?"

"Her house is up on top of it," Gatix said. "Where all people go sooner or later, and no one comes back. Even Grandfather Bear failed when he tried getting his son away from the Old Woman."

"Is that so?" Limper said.

"You don't know that story?"

Limper shook his head.

"I'll tell it to you, then," Gatix said. He got the winejug and refilled Limper's cup. Then he said, "This is the story of Grandfather Bear and the Old Woman." He spoke loudly and clearly, the way storytellers did.

"One day, Grandfather Bear's favorite son died. Grandfather Bear shut himself in his house and ate nothing and drank nothing for nine days. Then he said, 'I'm going to bring my son home,' and he got up and went out of his house and went up onto the Old Woman's Mountain. When he got to the Old Woman's House, he knocked on the door and said, 'Old Woman, Old Woman, you have my son. Open the door and let me in.'

"And the old Woman answered, 'Grandfather Bear, I have your son, but I won't open the door and let you in.'

"Then Grandfather Bear said, 'Old Woman, Old Woman, if you won't let me in, I'll beat on your door till I break it down.' And he beat on the door till the whole house shook, and the dead people inside it cried out in fright.

"Then the Old Woman said, 'Grandfather Bear, if you break down my door, all the dead people will get out and go back to their homes.'

"Grandfather Bear said, 'What do I care?'

"And the Old Woman said, 'Think of the men whose wives have died, and they have married again and have young wives to make them happy.'

"Grandfather Bear said, "It's true that you have my old wife in your house.'

"Then the Old Woman said, 'Think of the men

whose fathers have died, and now they sit in their fathers' chairs and eat the meat of fat lambs from their fathers' flocks.'

"Grandfather Bear said, 'It's true that you have my old father in your house. I hope he's doing well there, and that he's as happy as the dead can be.'

"Then the Old Woman said, 'Think of the men whose children died when they were babies, and now the fathers are old, and they say, if our children had lived we would have sons to guard our sheep and cattle and daughters to keep house for us. But no one gets any older in my house. If their children returned to them, they would still be babies.'

"Grandfather Bear said, 'It's true that many of my children died young. And I never did like babies.'

"After that Grandfather Bear turned around and went back down the mountain and left his son in the Old Woman's House."

When Gatix was done telling the story, Limper got up and moved back from the fire. By this time he was almost asleep.

Gatix said, "Do you want more wine?"

Limper nodded. Gatix got up and went across the room to get the winejug. Limper bent down and shook Nargri. She hissed, then opened her eyes. "This fellow makes me nervous," he said very softly. "Take a look around."

Nargri got up, muttering to herself in the language of the dragons, then went under a bench out of sight. "What's that sound?" Gatix said, turning around.

"I was talking to myself," Limper said.

"Your voice sounded different."

"I think I'm getting a cold."

Gatix brought the jug back and refilled the cups. Both of them drank. "Where are you going?" Gatix asked.

"To the northern lands."

"And where from?"

"Eshgorin."

Gatix said, "There was a fellow who stopped here who spent most of the night talking about Eshgorin. He said it was full of gold and silver. But he was from there, and he didn't have a copper penny to call his own."

"There are a lot of rich men in Eshgorin," Limper said, "and even more poor men."

"Do you want more wine?" Gatix asked.

Nargri returned from wherever she'd gone and went over to the cabin door. "I'd better let her out," Limper said. He got up and opened the door. Nargri went outside, turned and looked back at him. "I'd better keep an eye on her," Limper said. He went out after her and shut the door.

Snow was falling thickly; and the snow on the ground was so deep that Nargri had to stand up on her hind legs to keep her head above it. "There's a fellow in the back room," she said, "hanging by his heels, his throat cut. Part of his thigh is missing. It seems likely to me that was supper."

Limper felt as if he were choking. His stomach seemed to turn around inside him. After a moment he threw up.

Nargri said, "I won't say I haven't had better meals, but it wasn't that bad." Then she said, "I think Gatix is coming out.

Limper stopped retching, straightened up and turned. Gatix was standing in the doorway, an ax in his hand. "You're taking a long time," he said.

Limper pulled out his sword. Gatix started

toward him, wading through the snow, swinging the ax up, both hands on the haft. Limper stood waiting. When Gatix swung the ax down, he stopped it with his sword, his blade biting into the ax haft. Gatix pulled the ax away. For a moment the sword stayed stuck in the ax haft; Limper was pulled toward Gatix and had a hard time keeping hold of the sword. Then the sword came free, and he stumbled back. Gatix swung the ax down at him again. Again he stopped it with the sword. This time the blade met the axhead. Metal rang on metal. Limper felt the blow all along his arm.

"I've had guests before, who tried to be difficult," Gatix said and swung the ax up again. Limper stepped toward him and shoved the sword deep into his gut. Gatix grunted, then swung the ax down. Limper jumped back, letting go of his sword, which was stuck in Gatix. Gatix dropped the ax and grabbed ahold of the sword hilt, pulling the sword out of his gut. Then he turned it around and started toward Limper. Blood spurted out of the hole where the sword had been, soaking Gatix's shirt and pants and spattering the snow. Limper backed away from him, having a hard time moving through the snow. He groped for his knife, then got ahold of it and pulled it out of its sheath. Snow was blowing in his face, so he had trouble seeing. Gatix jabbed the sword at him. He stepped to one side and cut open Gatix's right arm above the wrist. Then Gatix turned and swung the sword at him as if he were swinging a scythe. Limper stepped back. After a moment he felt a stinging across his belly and looked down. His shirt was torn, and dark blood was coming out through the tear. Gatix said, "I don't understand how a man with a lame leg gets around as well as you do. But maybe you'll do less well now."

"That may be," Limper said.

Gatix jabbed the sword at him again. Again Limper stepped to the side. Gatix swung the sword toward him backhanded. Limper stepped closer to Gatix, so Gatix's arm hit him instead of the sword-blade. He reached over the arm and stuck the knife into Gatix's chest. Then Gatix grabbed Limper's shoulder with his free hand and gripped it hard, till Limper swore and let go of the knife and yanked himself free of Gatix's grip. Gatix pulled the knife out of his chest. He dropped it, then touched the place where it had gone into him. His hand came away covered with dark blood. "I think," Gatix said, "that was one cut too many." Then he looked down and saw the blood coming out of the wound in his gut and put his hand over the wound, trying to stop the blood. But it still came out. After a moment he dropped the sword and put his right hand over his left hand. Still the blood came out. The entire front of his shirt was dark with blood, also his pants and his right sleeve up to the elbow. He looked at Limper and said, "You didn't look like you'd cause me all this trouble." After a moment he fell to his knees. Soon after that he toppled over and was out of sight in the snow. Limper waited a while longer, then went over to him. Gatix was on his back, still alive, blood still coming out of him, running down his sides and darkening the snow. Limper looked around till he found his sword and picked it up. He put the sword point at the base of Gatix's throat, just above the collar bone, Gatix watching him while he did this. Then he shoved the sword down into Gatix's throat till he felt it hit the spine. Blood spurted out. Limper leaned on the sword until he felt it go through the spine. Then Gatix died.

Limper tugged at the sword till he got it free, turned and walked to the cabin, the sword in his hand. Nargri was sitting in the doorway. "Is he dead?" she asked.

Limper nodded and went past her into the cabin. He tossed down the sword, took off his shirt and looked at the wound in his belly. It wasn't deep but it was wide, and he had lost a lot of blood. His shirt and pants were soaked with it. He tore up his shirt and bound the wound with it, then he sat down on one of the benches. He felt dizzy and cold, and he was shaking too much to be able to stand. He looked at his trembling hands. There was blood on them, whose blood he didn't know, and they were so numb from cold that he had trouble clenching them. He closed them into fists, then opened them, then said to Nargri, "I'm going to ·sleep." He lay down on the bench. He heard Nargri close the cabin door and come over to him. Then he fell asleep.

When he woke, the fire in the fire pit was out. His belly hurt, and he felt hot and dry. He sat up. His shoulder, the one that Gatix had grabbed ahold of, hurt when he moved. Nargri was sitting at the end of the bench, watching him. "How are you?" she asked.

"Thirsty," he said. He stood up, then sat down again. "Get me some water."

She opened the door. She had trouble doing it, since the latch was almost out of her reach. Outside snow glittered in the sunlight. Nargri got a bowl and took it outside, going upright on her hind legs, her long tail balancing her, holding the bowl with her forefeet. She brought it back full of snow and gave it to him. He took a handful and rubbed it over his face and across the back of his neck. Then he ate the rest of it. When he was done, he lay down.

"Do you want something to eat?" Nargri asked. "There's some bread and some dried apples. I don't suppose you want to eat any more of that fellow in the back room."

"Leave me alone," Limper said.

Nargri shut the door. After a while Limper went back to sleep. When he woke up, he was cold. He sat up and looked around. The cabin was dark, and it was hard for him to make things out. "Nargri?" he called.

"Yes?" Her voice sounded muffled and seemed to come from a dark heap in one corner. He got up and went over to it. His belly and his shoulder ached, but he could get around without feeling he was about to faint. The heap was a fur cloak. He remembered it hanging on the wall. She had pulled it down onto the floor, so she would have some protection against the cold. She poked her head out from under the cloak and said, "I couldn't get the logs in here, Limper. They were too heavy."

"Where are they?" he asked.

"Outside the door."

He opened the door and went out. It was night. Snow was still coming down. Now it was hard and dry like grains of sand. There was a wind blowing, and he had no shirt on. He picked up two logs. When he bent over, the wound began to hurt. He went back inside and shut the door, then sat down on the floor, his back to the door, and rested a while. After that he built a fire. When he was done, he said, "Where are those dried apples you were talking about?"

"I'll get them," Nargri said. Limper sat down on a bench. He was feeling sick again. When Nargri brought him the dried apples, he said, "Did you see any clothes anywhere?"

"In the cellar," Nargri said. "I don't think Gatix ever threw anything away."

She went over to a trap door in the floor and pulled it open, slowly, with a great deal of effort. Then she went down a ladder. Limper ate an apple. He saw the wine jug he and Gatix had been drinking from, got it and drank a little wine. After a while Nargri came back up, holding a piece of green cloth against her chest with one forefoot. Limper took it and looked it over. It was a linen shirt with red embroidery around the neck, much too small for a man. A young boy must have worn it. He tore it up and used it to rebandage his wound. By now the fire was burning brightly, and the cabin was getting warmer, but he still felt cold. "Do you think we could share that fur cloak?"

"I suppose so," Nargri said.

He went and got the cloak. It was a bearskin, as intact as a bearskin could be, after having had the bear taken out of it. The head was still there and the paws with their long, curving claws, also the stubby tail. Limper lay down with the cloak over him. "I'm going back to sleep," he said. "Wake me in the morning. I have to see to the horses." After that he went to sleep. He woke some time later, when Nargri climbed onto the bench and crawled in under the cloak next to him. Then he went back to sleep.

The next morning Nargri woke him, and he went

out to the barn, wrapping the fur cloak around him. The sky was cloudless. The air was still and cold. The snow was thigh-deep, deeper in some places. He gave the horses water and hay, then went back to the cabin and breakfasted on stale bread and wine. Then he said, "What's in the cellar?"

"Almost everything," Nargri said.

Limper found a lamp and lit it and climbed down into the cellar, Nargri following him. He looked around. "It looks as if a lot of people left their belongings with Gatix." The cellar floor was covered with clothes and pieces of armor, jumbled together with saddles and bridles and saddlebags. He found a purse made out of fine red leather, half filled with silver coins, most of them minted in Eshgorin, and tucked it into his belt. Elsewhere he found a necklace made out of red gold, the links shaped like flowers. "I've seen better work," he said to Nargri, "but gold is gold." He put the necklace around his neck. In one corner, he found a toolbox containing all the tools a traveling smith would need. He took that up out of the cellar, then went back down and got himself some new clothes: a pair of woolen pants that were only a little too big for him, a blue linen shirt, and a woolen jacket. He took off his bloodstained pants and dressed himself, then picked up a silver gilt brooch he liked the look of. After that he went up the ladder.

He spent most of the rest of the day sleeping. When he woke late in the evening, he lit the lamp again and went back down into the cellar. He picked out a new saddle and a saddle bag big enough to hold Nargri, though she might feel somewhat cramped in it, and more clothes. He found a shield he liked well enough to take; and he looked for a mail shirt, but none of the ones he found came close to fitting him.

In the morning he saddled his horse and put the tool box, the extra clothes, and the rest of the food on one of the other horses. Then he said to Nargri, "I'm not leaving here till I make sure there really is a fellow in the back room." He went back into the cabin, into the back room. There was a man there all right, hanging by his heels, his throat cut. His shirt was gone, and one pants leg had been torn off. Most of that thigh was cut away. "Well, what happened to you?" Limper asked the man. "Did you go to sleep in this house and let Gatix cut your throat?" He looked the man over. He was young. His long hair was bright yellow, and his moustache was reddish-blond. There were scars on his face and arms. "You can't have been too bright," Limper said, then went back out to the barn. He lifted Nargri up into the saddle bag. "You weren't lying, were you."

"I'm very honest most of the time," Nargri said. "What was wrong with Gatix?"

Limper shrugged. "I don't know. Maybe he thought it was a waste to throw bodies out. This is poor country up here. People who live in places like this are usually provident."

"But why did he kill people?"

"To steal their belongings."

"I guess the old stories about men are right. You can always think up reasons to do harm."

Limper shrugged again. "Maybe." He untied all six horses, then led the two he was taking out of the barn. The other four horses followed. He went ahead of the horses, making a way through the snow. The day was cloudy and cold. The snow was knee-deep or deeper, and he went slowly, wading through it. Snow got into his boots and melted, and his feet got wet and cold and went numb, so he had trouble walking. The wound in his belly bothered him a little, but not much, and he didn't feel dizzy. After a while the snow grew less deep, and he mounted and rode. All morning the four other horses followed him. Early in the afternoon he started down out of the mountains. By late afternoon he was so far down that the snow was behind him except for a few patches in shady places. The four horses stopped to graze. Limper went on, leading his pack horse, leaving the four horses behind.

AMONG THE DRAGONS

The road they followed went down into valleys full of trees. Toward the end of the afternoon it began to rain. Limper found a cave, and they settled there to wait for the rain to stop. But the rain grew heavier, and a wind started to blow that whipped the branches back and forth, loosed the leaves and whirled them away. Nargri wandered around the cave. After a while she came back to where Limper was sitting at the mouth of the cave, with Gatix's fur cloak wrapped around him. She said, "There's a stone door at the back of the cave."

"Can you open it?"

"I tried. It's been blocked. It hasn't been used in a long time. There are leaves piled in front of it and bones left by whatever used to live in this cave."

"What?"

"Don't worry," Nargri said. "The bones are all dry, and the cave smells empty."

"How would you know that? Dragons don't have a good sense of smell."

"Well, maybe I'm wrong about the smell. But the bones are dry."

Limper grinned. "All right. I'll believe you."

They stayed in the cave till morning, then went on. The rain had stopped, though the sky was still grey and the ground still wet. When the wind shook the branches above them, drops of water spattered down on them. Ahead of them were steep hills, covered with forest. The road must have been dragon-built. Here and there the original surface still remained: slabs of stone with deep ruts worn in them. They forded a river beside a bridge that went halfway across, then stopped. Further on they came to a hundred-mile-stone, six feet tall with graffiti in half a dozen scripts on it. Limper made out the name 'Shogbor' in the dragon script and the words 'Grilya One Eye from Eshgorin wrote this'. The other inscriptions were in scripts he couldn't read. In the afternoon it started raining again. They made camp on top of a hill, in a thick grove where the ground was less wet than elsewhere. Limper built a fire and huddled close to it, trying to stay warm. Nargri slept in his arms, his cloak covering her. Toward morning the rain stopped, and by the time the sun came up, the sky was almost clear. To the west the snow-covered mountains shone in the sunlight. "Look," Nargri said and waved one of her forefeet. There were points of light glittering here and there on the white peaks: the glass roofs of dragon gardens.

They ate the last of the food from Gatix's house, then went on. The road still wound through narrow valleys and up around steep hills, going more-or-less north. They came to another bridge, this one going all the way across the river. On the other side of it a warrior waited, astride a big grey horse.

Limper reined his horse. "The hounds of hell take him," he said softly, "and tear him apart."

"Do you know that fellow?" Nargri asked.

"The horse is named Ghost, and he belongs to Enrin Silvershield. So it seems likely the man is Enrin. Get going, Nargri. See if you can find a stone door that's still open and get together a rescue party."

"Why don't you try to run, Limper?"

"Few horses can outrun Ghost. I don't think this nag is one of them. Get going."

Nargri dropped to the ground and went under a bush. Limper watched her till she was out of sight, then pushed his hair back from his face and smoothed his beard. After that he rode across the bridge. When he got to where the horseman was, he stopped. The horseman was bigger than most men, still young, and very handsome. His face was sunburnt dark brown, and his long, thick, curling hair was sun-bleached light brown, almost blond. Even in the middle of the wilderness, he was clean-shaven. His helmet, which had a gold lion on top of it, hung from his saddle horn. His silver-covered shield was slung across his back. His sword was in its gold-mounted scabbard. He looked at Limper, then smiled. "Good morrow, Holrin." His voice was deep and soft.

"I should have expected I'd meet up with you sooner or later, Enrin," Limper said.

"You know how the king values you."

Limper shrugged. "One trouble with kings, among the many, is when they like a man, they want to own him."

Enrin smiled again and nodded slightly. "I hear you made a sword in Hwara. May I see it?"

Limper pulled his sword out of its scabbard and handed it over, hilt first. Enrin took hold of it, shifted his grip slightly, then turned it this way and that, watching the pattern on the blade change. Then he said, "It's too bad soldiers know so little about language and poets so little about weaponry. I don't think your swords will ever get the praise they deserve."

Limper grinned. "I suppose, if you like the sword as much as you say you do, you aren't likely to let go of it."

"Will you promise me you'll give me no trouble going back to Eshgorin?"

"No."

"Then I'll keep the sword."

"I thought as much."

"I'd better have your knife, too."

"It's mediocre workmanship," Limper said, "not worth looking at."

"You had better give it to me, Holrin."

Limper shrugged, then handed him the knife, hilt first.

"We might as well start back now," Enrin said.

Limper nodded and turned his horse, recrossing the bridge with Enrin beside him. They rode for some time saying nothing. Then Limper said, "There's one thing I don't understand. How in hell did you get ahead of me?"

"I was behind you till I got to the mountains, and it started to snow. I thought you'd take shelter, so I kept going, thinking that I'd meet up with you. But I never did. After a while I began to think I must've passed you by."

"It's easy to miss things in the middle of a snow storm," Limper said.

Enrin nodded.

Every time they came to the top of a hill, Limper looked west toward the high mountains. At last Enrin said, "What are you looking for?"

"Smoke."

"You aren't likely to see any. What man would live up there?"

"None I know of," Limper said. "But dragons like to put their chimney tops where men can't get to them. They say that before they started doing that, men were always coming down their chimneys to steal their gold."

"I've never met a man who knew more about dragons than you do, Holrin."

Limper nodded. "Most men don't take the trouble to go out and meet dragons and talk with them, so all they know is old wives' tales. Which are wrong."

They stopped for the night where a brook ran under the road, through a stone duct. The brook was brimfull after so much rain, and the ground beside it was muddy. They made camp some distance away from it.

"I hope you have some food," Limper said.

"A little."

They ate what Enrin had: bread and dried beef and dried pears. Then Enrin said, "I'm going to have to tie you up, Holrin, since you won't give me your word."

Limper shrugged. Enrin tied his hands and feet. For a while after that Limper sat watching Enrin fiddle with his gear. Every time Enrin looked up, he was looking into Limper's eyes. Finally Enrin lay down to sleep, turning his back to Limper. After that Limper lay down, first on his side, then on his stomach. He had trouble getting to sleep. He was cold, and his wrists hurt, and he could find no comfortable position. At last, late at night, he dozed off.

He woke early, his hands numb and his wrists aching. Sunlight shone through the leaves above them, making the leaves glow. Enrin was still asleep, his sword and shield beside him. After a moment Limper saw the dragons. They waited without moving, in the green shadows at the clearing's edge. There were six of them, males, dark green with red or orange markings. They were as tall as men, standing upright on their hind legs, their tails balancing them. They wore mail shirts, the links gold-plated, and helmets with elaborate gold crests, obviously meant more for show than for battle. In their forefeet, which looked a lot like human hands, they held crossbows.

"Offer no resistance," one of them said in the language of the dragons.

"I wasn't planning to," Limper said in the same language.

Enrin woke and grabbed his sword.

"You'd better put that down," Limper said.

Enrin let go of the sword, then sat up. "What are they?"

"Dragons."

After a moment Enrin said, "Then there are such things. I didn't think there were."

The dragons came into the clearing. One of them picked up Enrin's sword; another picked up Limper's sword, which lay by the piled saddles and saddle bags; a third one cut Limper free.

"Gather your belongings and put them on the horses," the dragon who had spoken before said. He must have been the leader of the six. The crest on his helmet was the biggest and the most elaborate.

"Saddle Ghost," Limper said to Enrin.

The horses were moving restlessly, trying to pull free their tethers. Ghost stood still when Enrin told him to, but Limper had trouble getting the saddle on his horse and the pack on the pack horse. In the end Enrin helped him. When they were done, the dragon leader said, "Come with us."

They set off through the woods, Limper and Enrin leading the horses. Three dragons went ahead of them, and three followed behind. The dragons kept well away from the horses, but the horses were still uneasy and hard to manage. Limper couldn't handle both of his horses, so Enrin took the pack horse's reins and led it beside Ghost. They followed a winding path that went through narrow ravines and up over hills. The ravine bottoms were mirey, and the hillsides were steep and slippery, so it was hard going for the horses. At length they turned off the path and went up a hill into a cave. The cave was long and narrow and had a low roof. At its back was a stone door, so carefully set into the wall that it seemed part of the wall, until one of the dragons opened it. They went through the door into a second cave, so big and so dark that Limper couldn't see the roof or the far wall. The air was damp and cold and smelled of fish oil. Limper looked around. When his eyes got used to the darkness, he saw iron brackets set in the walls, with lamps in them. The dragons took the lamps out of the brackets and lit them. The smell of fish oil grew stronger. It was coming from the lamps. One of the dragons shut the stone door, and the dragon leader said, "Tie up the horses."

They tied the horses to iron rings set in the wall. Enrin said, "How long are we going to be here?"

"How should I know?" Limper said.

"Ask the dragons."

"How long are we going to be in your deep home?" Limper asked in the language of the dragons.

"Why ask us?" the dragon leader said. "Nobody ever tells a soldier what's going on."

"They don't know either," Limper said to Enrin.

"You'd better tell them to see to it that the horses get water and hay," Enrin said.

Limper repeated this to the dragon leader, and he nodded, then led the way out of the cave into a tunnel that sloped downward. The walls and ceiling and floor were smooth stone. There was no light except the lamps the dragons carried, no sound except the sound of their boots and the sliding, scuffling sound the dragons made walking. Twice they came to flights of stairs and went down them. On and on they went, always downward. Enrin strode beside Limper, his shoulders back and a slight frown on his face. From time to time he bit his lip. At last Limper heard the sound of water, the clanking of machinery and the wheezing of bellows. At first the sounds were barely audible, but they got louder and louder. They came from somewhere ahead. All at once the tunnel ended. Limper followed the dragons out into a cavern, onto the bank of an underground river. In front of them the river dropped, going over a dam. On the other side of the river was a big water wheel and beyond it three shaft furnaces that looked to be about fifteen feet high. Each furnace had two huge bellows attached to it, that filled and emptied, worked by the turning water wheel. The cavern was full of smoke and lit by the red light of the fires inside the furnaces.

Enrin said, "I thought it was dwarves who did such things."

Limper shook his head, but said nothing. It was too hard to talk through the sound of machinery. The dragons led them to a flight of stairs that went down beside the dam. They went down the stairs and along the river, till they came to where a raft was tied up. "Get on," the dragon leader shouted. They got on the raft, and the dragons followed them. One dragon untied the moorings. Two others put down their crossbows and their lamps and picked up long poles, pushing the raft out into the river. The other three dragons watched Limper and Enrin, holding their crossbows ready. Slowly the raft floated to the river's center, then moved slowly downstream away from the furnaces and around a bend. Looking back, Limper saw nothing of the furnaces except a red glow in the air and a red light on the water. Then that, too, was gone. The sound of machinery grew fainter and fainter. The cavern grew smaller till, on either side, the water lapped against the cavern walls and the cavern roof was just above their heads. Limper said, "The dragons say they've never met any dwarves, and they don't think there are any. They say men made them up to explain the dragon smithies they find from time to time."

"What do they intend to do?" Enrin asked.

Limper shrugged. "Who can understand the

heart of a woman, the mind of a dragon, or what fishes say to one another? That's a proverb I heard somewhere, or maybe I made it up."

Enrin frowned. "I never liked your jokes, Holrin."

After a while the cavern widened, and the roof rose so high that it was out of sight in the darkness. A dock built of stone stuck out into the river, lit by lamps on top of tall iron stands. The dragons poled the raft to it. They tied the raft up, then picked up their crossbows and lamps. Then they motioned the two men up the ladder onto the dock. The dragons followed after. When they were all on the dock, the dragon leader said, "That way," and waved at the flight of stairs, lit by lamps in brackets. They went up the stairs and along a corridor. At the corridor's end were two gold doors, decorated in high relief. On one door was a male dragon fighting a monster. On the other door there was a female dragon, her robe flying out as if the wind had caught hold of it, and waves curling around her feet.

"Shendil and Hro'ag," Limper said. "It's a famous love story."

"I didn't know the dragons told stories about love," Enrin said.

"They do."

The dragons pulled the doors open, and the dragon leader said, "Go in."

"Come on," Limper said to Enrin and went in through the doors, into a circular room. At the room's center three dragons sat on thrones. Limper stopped. The air in the room was cool and damp. It smelled of fish oil and of the musky odor of dragons. He looked around very briefly at the gold and silver tapestries on the walls. They showed forests full of monsters and dragon hunters armed with pikes and spears. He glanced up and saw dozens of hanging lamps. Then he looked at the dragons. Two were females, large and silver-grey. One wore a robe; the other wore a smith's apron made of asbestos. The third dragon was male, smaller than the other two and dark green with red streaks along his sides. He wore a mail shirt, a sword belt and a gold-hilted sword. Nargri was there, sitting on the floor in front of the three dragons. "Thanks for the rescue," Limper said to her.

"Don't thank me yet," she said in the language of Eshgorin.

"Introduce us, child," the dragon in the robe said.

Nargri said in the language of Eshgorin, "These are the three administrators: the Matriarch, the Captain and the Chief Technician."

Enrin and Limper bowed, then Limper looked to Enrin. "You first."

Enrin said, "I am Enrin Silvershield, the son of Ethvar the Traveler, the son of King Envar the Ill-Tempered, captain of the palace guard at Eshgorin, and the king's champion."

Nargri repeated this in the language of the dragons. Then Limper said in the same language, "Most people call me Limper. I can tell you who all my ancestors are, if you really want to know. But it seems to me you'd find the list even less interesting than I do."

"Your own name is enough," the Matriarch said. "We intervened in your quarrel because the child asked us to. We dragons won't last much longer if we don't help one another. But now we'd like to know what's going on. First of all, what are you doing with a dragon child?"

Nargri said, "I can answer that question. One of my aunts found Limper years ago, when he was still pretty young. She goes aboveground a lot."

"That's strange," the Captain said.

"My aunt says we dragons made a stupid mistake going underground. We should've stayed up in the open air and learned how to get along with men instead of fleeing into holes."

"Don't be ridiculous," the Chief Technician said. "Everyone knows men are impossible to get along with."

"That may be. Anyway, my aunt found Limper wandering around with no one to take care of him, since his father and brother had been killed, I forget how."

"Bandits," Limper said.

"So my aunt took him home and fostered him. He still comes back to visit her from time to time, now that he's grown up and lives among men. That's how I met him. It seemed to me he'd be a good person to travel with, and I wanted to see what the world was like aboveground. So the last time he came to visit, I went with him when he left."

"I'm surprised your mother let you go," the Matriarch said.

"I'm old enough to know my own mind," Nargri said. "And Limper promised my mother he'd take good care of me. Besides, my mother agrees with my aunt that it's stupid to hide in holes and leave the whole world's surface to men."

The Matriarch said, "I can't say I think what your mother did was right, but these days we

dragons can't afford to quarrel about anything."
She looked at Limper. "Why were you two men
quarreling?"

"That's simple enough," Limper said. "Enrin
works for the king of Eshgorin, as he told you, and
he's trying to take me back to the king. I don't
want to go."

The Captain said, "That may seem simple to
you, but not to me. Why is this fellow trying to take
you back to this king?"

"Why are you trying to take me back to Eshgorin?" Limper asked Enrin. "The dragons want to
know."

"The king told me to."

Limper translated this, and the Captain nodded.
"Soldiers ought to obey the orders their com-
manders give them. People with weapons and no
discipline are a great danger."

The Matriarch said to Nargri, "Child, tell us if
the man mistranslates anything, whether it's
something the other man says or something we
say."

"All right," Nargri said.

Then the Captain asked Limper, "Why does this
king want to get ahold of you?"

"I used to work for him. I didn't like the job, so I
left. And it looks to me as if he's unwilling to let
me go."

"What kind of work did you do?" the Chief
Technician asked.

"I'm a blacksmith for the most part, but I also
know how to work tin and copper and gold and silver."

The Chief Technician leaned forward. "Do you
have any samples of your work with you?"

Limper nodded. "The helmet Enrin's wearing,

also the shield across his back and his mail shirt. I also made his sword and mine, both of which your soldiers have."

The Chief Technician stood up and walked to Enrin, then walked around him. She came to a stop behind him and stared at the shield.

"What's it doing?" Enrin asked.

"She's looking at my smithwork," Limper said.

After a while the Chief Technician went back to her seat and sat down. "Why did you leave the king's employment?"

Limper frowned and stared past the dragons at the tapestry behind them. On it a horse with the head of a lion stood at bay, surrounded by dragon hunters. Finally he looked back at the Chief Technician. "For one thing, I don't really like working for other people. The king kept asking me to make toys: gold birds that whistled and snakes made out of links of gold, so they were as limber as living snakes, and so on. I'm not interested in things like that. And he likes gaudy weapons. To me, a weapon isn't any more useful inlaid with gold than it is plain, and a well-made blade doesn't need gold in it to look good. Also, he kept trying to hurry me, so I had a hard time doing a good job. If he'd had his way, I would have turned out a lot of junk with gold all over it." Limper shrugged. "After a while I got tired of arguing with him, so I left."

The Chief Technician nodded. "An artisan has an obligation to his or her art. It's not right to do slipshod work." After a moment she said, "It seems to me the best thing for you to do is kill the soldier. No one could blame him for not bringing you back, if he died trying to. And then you'd be free to use your skill as seems best to you."

"It isn't likely I'll try doing that," Limper said.

"Why not?" the Captain asked.

"For one thing, I'm not much of a fighter, and Enrin's very good at that kind of thing. I'd have no chance against him. Also, my father and his came from the same part of the world, so Enrin and I are countrymen. For all I know, we're kinsmen. Our fathers are dead, so we can't ask them about that. It's supposed to be terribly unlucky to kill a relative."

"Nothing is worse than a family argument," the Matriarch said. The Captain and the Chief Technician nodded.

"Why don't you hold onto Enrin for a few days? That'll give me time to get away."

The dragons shook their heads. The Chief Technician said, "The soldier will start after you as soon as we let him go, and if you two meet again you'll have the same problem to solve."

"I'll worry about that when it happens."

The Matriarch said, "Nothing is gained by postponing a problem. The best thing for you to do is solve it here and now, with our help. We dragons are very good at solving problems." She stood up. "We'll have to consult the three councils about this. Unless men are very different from dragons, you ought to be hungry. Go with the soldiers. They'll get you breakfast."

"We've been dismissed," Limper told Enrin. "Come on."

They bowed to the three dragons, turned and left the room, Nargri going with them. The dragon soldiers led them through corridors that branched and rebranched and were intersected by other corridors. Several times Limper heard the sound of rushing water somewhere close by; once he heard the clatter of machinery; and once he heard the sound of hammers. No smith made out of flesh and blood could bring a hammer down so regularly. It was the sound of the dragons' big hammers, worked by waterwheels. They met no other dragons. Enrin said, "This place seems almost empty."

Nargri said, "All deep homes do. There are far fewer dragons now than when the deep homes were dug."

"I wish I knew whether or not the Chief Technician liked my smithwork," Limper said.

"Couldn't you tell by looking at her?" Nargri asked.

Limper shook his head.

"Well, I could. She liked it."

Limper grinned. "Good."

At length the soldiers stopped at a door, opened it and showed them into a room where there was a table and chairs made out of iron. The walls were covered with tapestries woven out of gold and silver threads, which showed dragons fishing with nets. The soldiers left them. Enrin looked at Nargri, then said to Limper, "I heard in Hwara that you had what looked like a big lizard with you; and one fellow said it seemed to him that the lizard talked, though in a language he didn't understand. I thought the fellow was a liar or a lunatic. What were the dragons talking about at the end?"

"The Chief Technician suggested that I kill you."

"It—she did?"

Nargri said, "Limper said he couldn't, because you two might be kin."

"That doesn't seem likely to me," Enrin said.

"Nor to me," Limper said. "But I'm not going to

try to kill you, and that was the best reason I could come up with for not trying."

"Why aren't you going to try?" Nargri asked.

"For one thing, I'd probably fail. For another, Enrin is a hero; and there aren't many left. When one dies, it isn't easy to find a new hero to replace him. I don't want to be remembered for doing in one of the last members of a dying breed."

Enrin's face turned a little red. "That's as may be. Do you know now what the dragons intend to do?"

Limper nodded and grinned. "They intend to call the three councils together and solve our moral dilemma. There are two things dragons like more than anything else: technical problems and moral dilemmas."

Enrin opened his mouth to say something, but a dragon came in then, bringing a tray full of food. Enrin shut his mouth. The dragon set down dishes of baked fish and huge mushrooms that'd been stuffed and baked, pieces of thin, crisp bread and a bowl of what looked like translucent grey berries.

"What's that?" Enrin asked.

"Fish eggs." Nargri took a spoonful and put it on a piece of bread. "Have some."

Enrin shook his head. They sat down and ate. There was nothing to drink except water, which had a strong metallic taste.

"Don't the dragons have wine?" Enrin asked.

Nargri shook her head.

"They don't like any kind of alcohol," Limper said. "When they want to get drunk, they eat a certain kind of mushroom or burn an herb that they grow in their gardens and breathe the fumes from it."

"Oh." Enrin scratched his nose. "I suppose that's better than nothing."

After they were done eating and the dragon had taken the dishes away, Nargri said, "These dragons have been living by themselves a long time. They're not like my kinfolk. My kinfolk don't try to solve other people's problems for them. It's not polite."

"Well," Limper said, "maybe they can come up with a solution that'll make Enrin and me both happy. All we can do is wait and see." He pushed his bench back till he was able to lean against the wall behind him. "Tell Enrin the story about Shendil and Hro'ag. I don't think he believes the dragons make up stories about love."

"All right," Nargri said. "But I'm not sure I remember all of it." She scratched her snout, then settled herself more comfortably, her tail around her. "This took place long ago, when dragons lived above ground. There were dragons living by the sea; and they were troubled by a monster that came out of the sea every sixth night and broke down a house and ate whoever was inside it. When the dragons armed themselves and went after the monster, it fled into the sea where they couldn't follow.

"The dragons went to the dragon sorceress Shendil and asked her to help them, and she said she would. After which she went to the edge of the sea and gathered foam together and shaped it into a male dragon. She cut her arm and dripped blood onto the shape to give it life. It—I mean he— stirred and stood up and armed himself with the weapons she had brought for him. Shendil named him Hro'ag. From what the story says, he must've been very strange-looking. He was as white as sea foam, with bright red markings. But the story says he was beautiful.

"That night the monster came out of the sea, and Hro'ag met it. When the monster fled into the sea, Hro'ag followed it, for he was made out of the sea's substance and was able to live in the sea. The monster fled to a cave at the sea's bottom. Hro'ag followed it there and fought it and killed it. Then he returned to where Shendil waited on the shore.

"The story says it was sunrise then, and when Hro'ag came out of the sea and Shendil saw him, white as the surf he walked through, she fell in love with him.

"But sea foam isn't long-lasting stuff. As Hro'ag stepped onto the shore, he dissolved. Shendil cried out in horror. After which she gathered more sea foam together and remade Hro'ag and cut her arm again to give him life. He stirred, stood up and went with her to her house. They spent all day and all night together. But in the morning he dissolved as he had before. And she remade him.

"This went on for some time. Every morning Hro'ag dissolved and every morning Shendil remade him; and every day she grew weaker. The sea has more foam than we can measure, but there is only so much blood in a dragon. In the end Shendil died. And that's all there is to the story."

Limper said, "The story says she died in the morning. As Hro'ag stood up, she fell. He caught her, and she died with him holding her. He laid her on the sand and sat beside her all day and all night. In the morning he dissolved."

After a moment Enrin said, "It's a strange story."

"I don't like it," Nargri said. "She killed herself

because of something that wasn't real. That was stupid."

"It's pretty common," Limper said.

"That doesn't make it clever."

Enrin nodded. "That's true enough."

After a while a dragon came and took them to another room, where there were beds made out of iron with pads on them made of some kind of metallic cloth. This room had gold and silver tapestries which showed dragons tending plants in a dragon garden. The dragon showed them where the privy was at the end of the corridor. The chamber pot was fixed to the privy's floor, and there was a copper pipe going into it from a large copper cylinder behind it. Two more pipes went from the cylinder into the wall. On top of the cylinder there was a copper figure of a dragon holding a vase. The dragon who was showing them the privy turned a knob on the pipe going from the cylinder to the chamber pot. There was a gurgling noise, and water rushed into the chamber pot and out through a hole in the chamber pot's bottom.

"That's something I've never seen before or even heard about," Enrin said.

They used the privy and then went back to the bedroom. They had nothing else to do, so they put out the lamps and went to sleep. Nargri curled up next to Limper. He woke once, opened his eyes and saw absolute darkness. The room's air was still and smelled stale. He started up. Nargri stirred and hissed softly. "Sorry," Limper said.

"What is it?"

"I forgot where I was. Go back to sleep." He lay down again. Nargri snuggled against his side. After a while he went back to sleep.

He woke again when two dragons came in, one carrying a folding table and two folding chairs, the other carrying a lamp and food: more baked fish, more fish eggs, more bread and a preserve made from lemons. Enrin woke, sat up and looked around at the tapestries glimmering in the lamplight. "I don't think I'd like living underground."

"We didn't at first," Nargri said. "Or so the old stories say. But you can get used to almost anything."

When they were done eating, one of the dragons came back and took away the empty dishes. Sometime later the same dragon—an olive green fellow with orange markings—came back with another meal like the last. When they had eaten, the dragon said, "Come with me."

Enrin ran his hand over his jaw. "I should've brought my shaving gear in here with me. I don't like going around unshaven."

Limper said, "To these dragons, all men look strange and uncouth. They won't notice whether or not you've shaved recently."

The dragon led them through long corridors, then up a long flight of stairs and across a bridge. Looking over the parapet, Limper saw water far below, running between stone walls. On the other side of the bridge was a doorway. The doors, which were twenty feet tall and covered with gold, were open. The dragon said, "Go in."

Enrin stopped and frowned, then looked to Limper. "Why not?" Limper said.

They went through the doorway, down a ramp between stone walls and came out into the center of a circular theatre. They stopped there and Limper looked around. Three ramps came down to the stage and divided the theatre into three sections. Each section was divided in two by a central aisle; and in each section grey stone benches went up row after row to the back wall. There were twisting golden pillars there, that supported or seemed to support the roof, which was a gilt hemisphere. Golden lanterns hung down from the roof at the ends of chains. The lanterns were lit. They dimmed and flared overhead. Enrin looked around. "These dragons are skillful builders."

"You ought to see my home," Nargri said.

"She's right," Limper said. "This is a rabbit hole, compared to her home."

"Then they certainly must be great diggers there," Enrin said.

Dragons began to come into the theatre through doors at the back, behind the colonnade. They came down the aisles and seated themselves on the front benches: females wearing long grey gowns in one section, males wearing gold plated mail shirts in another section and, in the third section, males and females who wore smith's aprons or smocks. The dragons looked Limper, Enrin and Nargri over and talked softly to one another. Finally, when the theatre was half-full, no more dragons came in. After a moment Limper noticed the scent of dragons, strong and musky.

Enrin wrinkled his nose. "Pah. What a stink."

"I like it," Limper said. "It reminds me of my childhood."

Enrin shrugged. "Do you know what this is about?"

"It looks to me like a meeting of the three councils," Limper said.

"That doesn't tell me much."

"We dragons don't have kings," Nargri said. "Instead we govern ourselves. Every deep home has three councils, which set policy, and three administrators, who handle everyday problems. The administrators are elected by the three councils: the Matriarch by the Council of Matrons, the Captain by the Council of Soldiers and the Chief Technician by the Council of Technicians. Every grown-up dragon belongs to one of the three councils."

Enrin looked around the theatre. "There aren't more than two hundred dragons here. Are these all the grown-up dragons in this city?"

Nargri said, "I think this is a meeting of the lesser councils. They handle problems that are too important for the administrators, but not important enough for the great councils."

A moment later the three administrators entered, each one coming down a different aisle to three seats that had been left unoccupied, one in each section in the front row on the aisle. The dragons stopped talking and sat still. The Matriarch said, "We have arrived at a solution." Then she said, "As far as we can see, the only way to settle this so the smith doesn't have to misuse his skills and the soldier doesn't have to disobey his orders is for one of them to die. But since they may be kinfolk, neither can kill the other. Therefore our solution is this: we dragons will kill one of the two."

After a moment Limper asked, "Which one?"

"We haven't decided that," the Matriarch said. "It seems to us the best way to decide that is for you to throw dice."

"I'll have to tell Enrin this," Limper said. Then he said in the language of Eshgorin, "They've come up with a solution to our problem."

"What is it?"

"They're going to kill one of us."

"I can't say I care for that solution. I think it's time we got out of here, Holrin."

Limper nodded.

Enrin said to Nargri, "What about you, little one?"

"I'm not staying here. It's my opinion these dragons have been living on their own so long that they've gone crazy."

Limper said in the language of the dragons, "Your solution sounds fair enough, but today is a holy day for us. Gambling on such a day is a sin, so we can't throw dice now."

"Then we'll wait till tomorrow to finish with your problem," the Matriarch said. "The other problem is the child Nargri. It seems to us she should stay here, among her own kind. The world above ground is too dangerous, and she'll never get a decent education, if she stays among men."

Nargri was sitting right beside Limper. She pressed herself against his leg, and he felt her shaking. He looked down at her. "Keep calm."

"What right do these turtles have to decide my life for me?" she said in the language of Eshgorin.

"What did you say, child?" the Matriarch asked.

Limper said, "She was telling me good-by."

"You'll have time to do that properly, child. Don't worry." The Matriarch rose. A moment later the Captain and the Chief Technician rose too, and the three of them went out of the theatre, each one the way he or she had entered. The other dragons stamped their feet and hissed loudly.

"What's that about?" Enrin asked.

"They're showing they approve of what's happened," Nargri said.

The dragons started leaving the theatre, talking to one another noisily. "We might as well wait," Limper said. "I don't like pushing through crowds."

When the theatre was almost empty, Enrin said, "Do you want to make a run for it now, Holrin?"

Limper shook his head. "Let's wait a while and see if our chances get any better. I don't think they can get any worse."

They went out the way they'd come in. Four soldiers waited at the gold doors. They were armed with spears and shields instead of crossbows, and gold-hilted swords hung at their sides.

"You see?" Limper said in the language of Eshgorin. "We wouldn't have gotten far."

"Please come with us," one of the soldiers said.

Limper nodded.

The soldiers took them back to the bedroom where they'd been before. "We have till tomorrow," Limper said as soon as they were alone. "Though I'm not sure how long that is. I find it difficult to tell time underground." He scratched his chin and frowned. "I want quiet for a while."

"All right," Enrin said.

Limper lay down on one of the beds, his hands behind his head, and looked at the ceiling. Like the floor and the walls, it was dark, smooth stone.

Some time later a dragon came in with food: more fish, more fish eggs, more bread and a big jug of metallic tasting water. The soldiers kept watch outside the open door, holding their spears ready. The dragon put the dishes down, then went out, and the soldiers shut the door. Limper got up and spooned fish eggs onto a piece of bread, then ate the bread. "All I can think of is I'd sooner be in Eshgorin than here."

"I wish you'd decided that earlier," Enrin said.

Later Limper tried to open the door. It was locked. He knocked on it, and a voice said, "What do you want?"

"I want to use the privy."

The door was opened, and he went out into the corridor. There were only two dragon soldiers left on guard, both armed with spears and swords. "Go on and use it," one of them said.

Limper went down the corridor to the privy. One of the soldiers followed him and waited for him outside the privy. While he was in it, he stepped up onto the rim of the chamber pot and took a closer look at the copper figure on top of the water tank. It was bolted in place. He braced his arms against the tank top and tried to pull the figure free, but he wasn't able to budge it. He stepped down onto the floor and turned the knob to let water into the pot.

When he got back to the bedroom, he said to Enrin, "The figure in the privy on top of the tank, do you remember it?"

Enrin nodded.

"It's bolted down, and I can't move it, but you're supposed to be stronger than most men."

"If I can get it free, what do you want me to do with it?"

"Leave it where it is. I'll think of a use for it," Limper said.

Enrin nodded again.

Sometime later Enrin told the dragon soldiers that he had to use the privy. They let him out.

When he came back and the door was shut, he said, "The figure's no longer bolted down. Now it's up to you to think of a way to use it."

"All right," Limper said.

"Do you really have a plan?" Nargri asked. "Because if you do, you'd better discard it. None of your plans have worked so far."

Enrin laughed.

Limper lay back down and looked at the ceiling, his hands behind his head.

"Aren't you going to answer her, Holrin?" Enrin asked.

"No." After a while Limper said, "I'm going to see if I can do something about one of those soldiers. You'll have to see to the other one."

"All right," Enrin said.

Limper got up, rapped on the door and told the soldiers he needed to use the privy again. They led him out, and one of the soldiers said, "I know nothing about men, but if you were a dragon, I'd say you were nervous."

Limper shrugged and said nothing. As before one of the dragons went with him to the end of the corridor. Limper went into the privy and shut the door. The copper figure's flat base was twisted, so it no longer stood upright but tilted to one side. Limper took hold of it and lifted it. It came away from the tank easily. It was about a foot and a half long, hollow but nonetheless heavy. He held it behind him, opened the door and said, "I turned the knob and nothing happened."

The soldier said, "I've heard that men are worse than useless around machines, however simple. Let me take a look at it."

He went past Limper into the privy. Limper looked down the corridor. The other soldier was close to the door of their bedroom, one hand on the latch. He looked to the soldier in the privy. He was bending down to turn the knob, and the back of his neck was bare, protected neither by his helmet nor by his mail shirt. Limper brought the figure down on the soldier's neck. He shut the privy door as the soldier began to fall. The soldier's spear clattered against the wall, and his metal scabbard clanked against the floor. His armored body hit the chamber pot, and he ended sprawled across it. Limper put the copper figure down, then pulled the soldier over on his side. He unbuckled the soldier's sword belt, took it off him and buckled it around his own waist. He had cut the soldier when he hit him; and blood seeped out of the cut and dripped onto the floor. He picked up the soldier's shield. The arm-band and the handgrip were in the wrong places, so that it was hard to hold, but it was better than nothing. He paused a moment. "Good luck to me," he said out loud. He opened the privy door and went into the corridor. There was no one in sight. He hurried down the corridor and rapped on the door to their bedroom.

"Who is it?" Nargri asked.

"Limper."

The door opened. He went inside. The second dragon soldier was there, lying on the floor. Enrin had the soldier's sword in his hand.

Nargri said, "Enrin strangled him."

"So I see," Limper said.

"I told the soldier I didn't want to be with men anymore. I asked him to let me out. He opened the door, and Enrin grabbed ahold of him. I'm feeling sick, Limper."

Enrin said, "More than one dragon may come to harm, before we get out of here."

"To say nothing of what may happen to us," Limper said.

"So you still want to come with us, little one?" Enrin asked.

"Yes. I suppose it serves them right for trying to solve other people's problems."

Enrin took the dragon soldier's sword belt off him and put it on, then put the dragon sword into its scabbard. "It's a good enough sword, but I don't like leaving Lionstooth behind. Do you know where they would put it, little one?"

"The armory, most likely. Though they might put it on display in the museum."

"You aren't thinking of going after it?" Limper asked.

Enrin said nothing.

"If the two of us get out of here, I'll make you a new sword as good as Lionstooth."

Enrin grinned. "I'll remember that promise, Holrin." Then he put on his helmet, took hold of his shield and picked up the dragon soldier's spear. "You'd best go first, little one."

"All right," Nargri said.

They went out of the bedroom, Nargri going first, Limper after her, Enrin last. The corridor was empty. Nargri said, "I know only one way out: the way we came in."

"Get going," Limper said.

She led them down the corridor. Limper stopped in the privy to get the spear there. The soldier hadn't moved. Blood was still dripping from the wound on his neck, and there was a little pool of it on the floor. At the corridor's end Nargri turned into another corridor and when this divided, she went to the left. She moved quickly, and Limper had trouble keeping up with her. They went through one corridor after another, all alike: smooth dark stone walls and floor and ceiling. Every thirty or forty feet there was a lamp in an iron bracket, burning dimly. For a while there was no noise except their footsteps. Then Limper heard the sound of hammers and the sound of water. Nargri came to an intersecting corridor, looked either way, and stopped. Limper and Enrin stopped some ten paces behind her. She stared at the right-hand corridor. The two men moved against the right-hand wall. A moment after they did that, three dragons dressed in aprons came out of the right-hand corridor. One said, "Child—" then stopped and looked at the men.

"Stand still and keep quiet," Limper said.

The dragons ran, one going across the corridor into the corridor opposite, the other two turning back the way they'd come. All three were yelling.

Enrin said, "I think from here on we'd better hurry."

They went on, moving even more quickly. Enrin was beside Limper now, slowing every few steps so he wouldn't leave him behind. Several times Nargri stopped and waited till they caught up with her. Limper's bad leg was beginning to bother him. He heard the sound of gongs behind them, first a small gong that was being hit rapidly and unevenly, then the slow, even *bong-bong-bong* of a big gong. The sound echoed in the corridor.

They came to a flight of stairs going up. Nargri stopped at the foot of it and waited. When they got to her, Limper said, "I don't remember this."

"It shouldn't be here," Nargri said.

"Since it is, we'd better go up it," Enrin said. "Or so it seems to me."

Limper nodded, and they started up. The sound

of the gongs got fainter and fainter until he couldn't hear it anymore. Nargri reached the top of the stairs well ahead of them, stopped and looked back down. There was a lamp right above her. Her dark scales gleamed in the light and her eyes, orange with slit pupils, shone. The stairway was narrow, and Enrin was behind Limper, only two steps back. By this time Limper's bad leg was beginning to ache, and the wound in his belly hurt. Maybe it was infected. He should have changed the bandage. At the top of the stairs there was a corridor that sloped up. Nargri turned and scurried on ahead of them.

This part of the dragons' home looked little-used. There were few lamps burning, and those few were long distances apart, so the tunnel was always dim and often dark. Most of the side corridors were unlit. Limper heard water once, a soft, trickling sound that came out of a side corridor, but he heard no more hammers or machines. At last they came to a place where the corridor divided into three. Left and right the corridors ran level and were lit, but in front of them a flight of stairs went up into darkness.

"Well?" Limper said.

"The stairs seem best to me," Nargri said. "I'm not sure, but I think we're still deep underground."

"All right." Limper reached up to take a lamp from its bracket.

"If you take that, they'll know which way we went," Nargri said.

"You want us to go up there without a light?"

"Yes."

"All right," Limper said. "But you go first, and if

you fall off a precipice, shout so we'll know that the way gets dangerous."

"All right," Nargri said, and she started up. Limper and Enrin followed. The stairs went straight up with no turns and no landings. They were soon in darkness. For a while when he looked down, Limper saw the light at the bottom of the stairs. Then that was out of sight. He could see nothing. He kept one hand on the wall and followed the sound of Nargri's footsteps. Behind him Enrin was beginning to breathe heavily. He heard the soft chink-chink of the chains that held their scabbards to their sword belts. All at once he heard a new sound and stopped. Enrin bumped into him. "What is it?" Enrin asked.

"Limper?" Nargri said somewhere ahead of him.

"Shut up," Limper said.

The sound was the sound of footsteps below them, coming up the stairs. "They seem to have found us," Limper said, speaking softly.

"They must be searching every corridor," Nargri said.

Enrin said, "We'd better keep going."

They went on. A little while later Limper looked back and saw a point of light behind and below them. He kept climbing the stairs, Nargri ahead of him, Enrin behind. His bad leg was aching from ankle to thigh, and he was short of breath. He looked back again. It seemed to him the light was brighter, and the footsteps sounded louder. At last he stopped, and Enrin bumped into him again. Limper said, "You go on, if you want to. I'm staying here. I can't move quickly enough to get away from those fellows."

After a moment Enrin said, "I'd better be the

one to stay. I'm faster than you are and a better fighter. I can deal with the dragons, then catch up with you."

"All right," Limper said.

"Give me your spear."

Limper held out his spear. Enrin was closer than he thought. He scraped his knuckles on his mail shirt. Enrin took hold of the spear. "You'd better get going, Holrin."

Limper went on, Nargri ahead of him. Soon he looked back. The light was a lot closer. He could see moving figures lit by it and the dark, still shape of Enrin. Limper kept on climbing, going as quickly as he was able. His leg hurt badly, and he was gasping for breath. Then he heard someone shriek. He stopped and looked back. The light had gone out.

"We can't stop, Limper," Nargri said. They went on.

A moment later he heard someone running up the stairs. He pulled his sword from its scabbard. When whoever it was was closer, Limper stopped and turned. "Who is it?"

"Enrin."

Limper sheathed his sword, and they kept going up the stairs. From time to time Limper looked back. He saw no light. But he could still hear footsteps. They seemed to be following more slowly than before.

Ahead of him Nargri said, "The stairs stop."

"Good," Limper said. The wall he was touching turned a corner. He slid his foot forward, and it didn't come up against another step. He stood still and waited. Enrin stopped beside him, his shield touching Limper's arm.

"What's there, little one?" Enrin asked.

After a moment Nargri said, "It's a room. It isn't very big." Then she said, "I've gone all the way around it. There aren't any doors out of it."

Limper looked back. He could see the light again, far below.

Nargri said, "There must be a stone door, but I can't find it."

"Keep looking, little one," Enrin said. "Holrin and I will see to these dragons."

"It seems to me the best thing I can do is to stay out of your way," said Limper.

Enrin laughed. "I think there'll be enough dragons to keep both of us busy, Holrin."

"Oh, all right." Limper turned so he was facing the light and pulled his sword from its scabbard. "Are you looking for the door, Nargri?"

"Yes."

"We'd do well to get away from the stairs," Enrin said. "The dragons have crossbows."

"All right." Limper moved to one side of the stairs, feeling his way along the wall, then stopped and waited. At first he wasn't able to see anything. He heard Nargri moving around and the sound of Enrin's breathing and his own, loud and fast at first, then slower and less noisy; and he heard the dragons coming up the stairs, their feet scraping and scuffling on the stone steps. After a while he could make out the doorway at the top of the stairs. The light brightened. He could see the glimmer of Enrin's armor opposite him, on the other side of the doorway. The footsteps stopped. Somewhere below him a dragon said, "They can't have opened the door. We would've seen the light."

"Unless it's night above ground," another dragon said.

"In any case, it's possible that they're at the top

of the stairs," said the dragon who had spoken first. "We have two choices. Either we can wait here till reinforcements come or we can go on up."

One of the other dragons said, "You'll have to talk a long time before you'll convince me to go up there."

Limper looked around for Nargri. He could see her now, sitting and looking at the room's back wall. After a moment she stood up on her hind legs and felt along the wall. Finally she stopped and pushed against the wall. A rectangular section swung back away from her. Sunlight came in, so bright that for a moment Limper was blinded.

One of the dragons said, "That's done it. We can't wait any longer."

Enrin said, "You go ahead."

By this time Limper could see again. He saw Enrin step to the top of the stairs, holding his shield in front of him. He still had one spear.

"Come on," Nargri shouted.

Limper went out the door after her, up another flight of stairs. A crossbow bolt whished past him, over his right shoulder. He got to the top of the stairs. He was at one end of a long, stone building roofed with glass and full of sunlight. An aisle went the length of it between tables on which there were dwarf lemon trees. The lemons were bright yellow, as big as the lemons from full-sized trees; and the branches were propped up so they wouldn't break. Nargri ran down the aisle to the door at the other end. Limper followed her. She got to the door well ahead of him, went up on her hind legs, turned the knob and started to pull the door open. Then Limper got to the door and pulled it the rest of the way open, knocking Nargri backwards as he opened it. Snow spilled in. In front of him was a wide field of snow, bright in the sunlight. Beyond it he saw the peaks of mountains. He looked back. Enrin was half way down the aisle, moving sideways, his shield between him and the dragons. He no longer had the spear. The dragons were coming up the stairs into the garden. Limper looked for Nargri, grabbed her up and got out the door. The snow was knee deep. He stepped to one side of the door, then set Nargri down and said, "I think there's going to be a fight. Find somewhere safe."

"I'd've been safer inside. I'll freeze out here."

"Then go back in," Limper said.

"I will," Nargri said. She started in the door. Enrin, coming out, tripped over her and fell face down in the snow. Nargri shrieked and scurried in through the door. Limper swore, then stepped over Enrin into the doorway. The dragons were half way down the aisle. There were three of them, armed with crossbows. One stopped to shoot at him. The bolt hit his shield and bounced off it. The other two dragons were still coming toward him.

"You'd better slow down," Limper said in the language of the dragons. "The hasty come soon to harm."

The first dragon stopped, and the second dragon bumped into him. "He's right," the first dragon said.

Out of the corner of his eye, Limper saw Enrin get up on his hands and knees, grab his shield, then stand. One of the dragons lifted up his crossbow. Limper said in the language of Eshgorin, "Get to the side." He stepped out of the doorway and against the building's wall. Enrin got to the wall on the other side of the doorway. His face was covered with snow, as was the front of his mail shirt. The front part of the lion crest atop his helmet was encased in a glob of snow. Limper grinned. "The court ladies of Eshgorin ought to be here to see you."

Enrin wiped the snow off his face. "I wouldn't mind, so long as they brought their menfolk with them. It seems to me we're going to need help."

Limper nodded. "I don't think they'll come out after us for a while." He looked around and saw another dragon garden, so far away that all he could make out was a glittering line of light. Aside from that, there was nothing in sight except snow and the cloudless sky and snow-topped peaks that looked to him as if they were a long way off. He said, "If they do come out, you'll have to see to them. I'll be back." He started around the building. The snow was sticky and wet. By the time he'd gotten half way around the building, his pants were soaked up to the knee and he had water in his boots. In back of the building the land rose, and there were boulders capped with snow, outcroppings of rock, steep slopes and a sheer, bare cliff. On the other three sides snow-fields stretched long distances. Beyond them there were mountains. He was getting cold. The wound in his belly still ached, and the glare off the snow hurt his eyes. "All my luck is bad," he said as he looked at the snow fields.

When he was most of the way around the building, he heard someone yell. He hurried back to the door. Enrin was standing there, cleaning his sword blade with snow; and there was blood on the snow close by him. The door into the dragon garden was shut. Enrin looked at Limper. "I heard them moving around in there and talking in their language. I kept quite. After a while one of them stuck his head out."

"It looks as if he was well enough afterward to get back inside," Limper said.

Enrin shook his head. "The others dragged him back. Where's the little one?"

"Inside. It's too cold for her out here, and they won't hurt her, the folk in there. The land goes up behind the building, but it seems to me we ought to go down. And I don't know where to go to do that."

Enrin said, "We might as well go straight ahead." He frowned. "Do you want to try to get the little one out of the building?"

Limper shook his head. "She's safer where she is. We're not likely to get out of this."

Enrin nodded, then put his sword into its scabbard and started away from the building. Limper sheathed his sword too and followed Enrin. The snow deepened quickly, till it was thigh-deep, and they had a hard time getting through it. More snow got into Limper's boots and melted. His feet grew numb. After a while the land sloped up. The snow was less deep here, and they moved more quickly. Enrin turned to the right, so they were no longer going directly toward the other dragon garden. But the land sloped steeply down, and they were soon waist-deep in snow. Enrin turned back toward the dragon garden, then tried turning to the left. Again the land sloped, and the snow got deep; and Enrin turned back toward the dragon garden. They tried several times to change direction, going first to one side, then to the other. Each time they ended in deep snow. They were on a ridge that went from one dragon garden toward the other, and when they left it they ended in drifts. The ridge was going slowly upward, getting more and more narrow. Each time they tried to turn to the side, they were able to go a shorter distance than before. Limper kept looking back. At last he saw four small, dark figures beside the dragon garden: the dragon soldiers had come outside. He looked back again a moment or two later. The dragons had started after them. "Take a look behind," he said.

Enrin stopped and looked back. "It took them longer to come out than I expected." Then he went on, Limper following.

The ridge stopped rising and ran level. The snow was ankle-deep. By this time Limper was feeling very cold, and the glare off the snow had given him a headache. He kept his head down and looked at his own shadow as much as possible.

Enrin said, "I think we'd better make another try at changing our direction."

Limper looked up. They were close enough to the second dragon garden so he could see it clearly: a long, one-story, grey stone building with a steep pitched glass roof. In front of the building were six dragons.

Enrin turned to the right, going down off the ridge. The snow was soon thigh-deep. They went slowly, Enrin going first, making a path, and Limper following in the path he made. By this time Limper's boots were full of snow to their tops. His belly and his bad leg both hurt, and he was shaking from cold. He looked back and saw the dragons on the ridge top, moving from either side toward the point where Enrin and he had left the ridge.

The land rose a little, and the snow was only knee-deep The four dragons from the lemon-tree

garden were still a long way off, but the six
dragons who'd come out of the other garden were
starting down off the ridge on the path Enrin had
made. Limper heard something whish past him
and saw a crossbow bolt go into the snow ahead of
him.

"You'd better go first," Enrin said. "My armor
may be able to stop a bolt. I know your shirt
won't."

"All right." Enrin stopped, and Limper went
past him. As he did so, Enrin winced. "What is it?"
Limper asked.

"Nothing," Enrin said. "Go on."

Limper started through the snow. After a moment he realized Enrin wasn't keeping up with
him. He stopped and looked back. Enrin was
standing still. Half a crossbow bolt stuck out of his
thigh, and blood darkened his pants leg around the
bolt. "You had better go on," Enrin said.

"I'm pretty sure I won't get out of this alive, no
matter what I do." He went back to Enrin, put an
arm around him and helped him walk. After they'd
gone a few steps, Limper looked back at the
dragons. They were getting close. "If we do a good
enough job of dying, maybe the dragons will tell
stories about us."

Enrin laughed. "We're all alike, we
northerners."

"I'd hate to think that," Limper said.

They were going very slowly now. Limper
looked back again. Two of the dragons were still
on the path that he and Enrin had made. The other
four had left it, two going to the left and two going
to the right.

"Will you tell me something, Enrin? I don't
want to die full of curiosity."

"Yes?"

"Why did you come after me? I can't believe the king couldn't find another smith."

"He sent me," Enrin said. "But he had more than one reason."

"I thought as much." Limper looked around. The dragons were closer.

"There was no war on, so I was at court. All those fine little lordlings there were making me edgy. They're like walking bouquets, Holrin—sweet-smelling and brightly-colored, oh so pretty. I was getting ready to challenge one to a duel, when the king decided to send me after you."

Limper laughed, then nodded. "That makes sense to me."

They kept on till the dragons who had left the path were on either side of them, maybe forty feet away. Limper looked back. The dragons on the path were forty or fifty feet behind them. The dragons all carried crossbows, and they all wore jackets and pants and snow goggles. Even their tails were covered by something that looked like a third pants leg.

"We might as well stop," Limper said.

They stopped. Enrin said, "I can stand by myself."

Limper let go of him, and Enrin drew his sword, saying, "It isn't likely this will be of any use. They'll probably stay where they are and shoot us."

Limper nodded, then drew his sword. They both turned, so they were back to back. The dragons that Limper faced moved a little closer, but they didn't raise their crossbows. After a moment Enrin said, "I was right. They're going to shoot."

A moment after that Limper felt Enrin fall

against him. He turned and caught Enrin before he fell further. There was a crossbow bolt deep in Enrin's forehead, and he was dead. Limper lowered him into the snow, then straightened up. The dragons turned and started back the way they'd gone. "Where in hell are you going?" Limper asked.

One of them said, "Inside. It's cold out."

"You're leaving me here?"

"We're certainly not going to take you with us. You men are too violent for our liking."

Limper watched the dragons till they reached the ridge. The dragons from the other dragon garden were there, waiting. Together they went back toward the garden full of lemon trees. Limper put his sword back into its scabbard, then bent and closed Enrin's eyes, which were light brown, almost yellow. The lashes were very fair, he noticed, as was the stubble on Enrin's chin. The stubble glinted in the sunlight like white gold. He set to work covering Enrin's body with snow, so the carrion birds wouldn't be able to get to it, for a while anyway. When he was done, he squatted a moment, looking at the mound of snow. He shook his head. "Heroes don't live long, Enrin. I expected to outlive you. But I didn't expect you to die in a lonely place like this. I thought you'd die in the sight of armies." He stood up. "This isn't right, somehow." He looked around at the bright fields of snow. "Well, goodbye. I hope, for your sake, there's an afterlife." He turned away, going back along the path he and Enrin had made. There were no dragons around that he could see. He was shivering, and his leg hurt so much it was hard to walk. When he reached the ridge, he started toward the second dragon garden, the one he and

Enrin had been heading for. The snow wasn't deep, and the dragons had made a wide path through it. A wind started to blow. He tucked his hands under his arms and kept on. It didn't take him long to get to the garden. He opened the door, fumbling at the knob with numb fingers, and went inside. The building was full of yellow wheat. A gust of wind blew in the open door. The wheat-stalks swayed back and forth, making a faint rustling sound. He shut the door, then went down the aisle to the door into the dragons' home. The door was shut, and he couldn't open it. After a while he gave up trying and sat down, his back against the shut door. The sun was no longer directly overhead, and along one wall there was a shadow, but most of the wheat was still in sunlight. The wound in his belly was still bothering him. He took off his shirt and undid the bandage, then looked at the wound. It had completely closed, and the flesh on either side of it was white, not red. He poked at it. It didn't hurt that much. "Well, it could be worse," he said. He redid the bandage and put his shirt back on.

He stayed where he was till he felt warm. Then he got up, went outside and started back to the first dragon garden. The wind was stronger than before, but he got to the garden before he was too cold. He went inside, shutting the door behind him, walked down the aisle between the lemon trees, and tried to open the garden's second door, into the dragons' home. He couldn't. "There are times I really wish I'd stayed in Eshgorin," he said out loud. He picked a lemon, pulled out his sword and cut the lemon in two, then ate it slowly, sucking out the sour juice and chewing the pulp. When he was done, he tossed away the rind. He looked around.

There were iron grates set in the floor. Far below them he saw fires burning. He tried to lift one of the grates up, but he wasn't able to. It was fixed in the stone. There was a tool box at the back of the building. He went to it and opened it. Inside were a pair of shears, a trowel, and a rake with a short handle. He looked these over, then shrugged and put them back in the box and closed it. There was nothing else in the building except the tables and the lemon trees. He sat down in the aisle beside one of the grates and scratched his chin. "Well, what next?" The air coming out of the grate was warm. He started to get sleepy. He lay down, his hands behind his head, and looked up through the garden's glass roof at the bright, cloudless sky. After a while he went to sleep. When he woke, it was dark. Most of the glass roof was misted over, but right above the grate there was a spot where the glass was still clear. He lay looking up through the clear spot at the stars. He was hungry, he had a headache and he felt as if he might be getting a cold. He got up finally and picked another lemon, cut it open, and ate it. Then he lay down again and went back to sleep.

When he woke, the sky was dawn-grey. He heard a noise, sat up and looked around. The door into the dragons' deep home was open. Nargri was coming down the aisle toward him. She stopped. "Are you all right, Limper?"

"I didn't expect to see you again. Where've you been?"

"I went in through the stone door when the dragons were out chasing you and Enrin. I thought the best thing I could do was to find a way out."

"Did you find one?" Limper asked.

"Yes."

"Then let's go." Limper stood.

"What happened to Enrin?" Nargri asked.

"They killed him. They didn't even try to kill me, and I'd like to know why."

"You didn't learn much while you lived with my aunt. It seems to me sometimes that you know practically nothing about dragons. The three councils decided to kill one of you. If the soldiers had killed both of you, they would've been killing one without the council's authorization, which would have been murder and mutiny."

"Why'd they pick Enrin?"

"I'm not sure," Nargri said. "Probably because he seemed more dangerous than you. They had to leave one of the two of you up here alive. They probably thought it'd be safer to leave you. Enrin might've figured out a way to get away."

"They left me up here to die?" Limper asked after a moment.

"Yes."

"And that's not murder."

"Letting someone die isn't the same as killing them," Nargri said.

"I don't see much difference, but then I've never studied any law, or philosophy either, for that matter. I suppose distinctions like that make sense to lawyers and philosophers."

"Yes," Nargri said. "Should I have stayed with you and Enrin, Limper? There was nothing I could do, and I would've frozen out there."

"Don't worry about it."

"It's wrong to leave friends when they're in trouble."

Limper shrugged. "If you think you can get through life without doing anything wrong, you're crazy. Now get me out of here. Those dragons are going to start wondering what happened to you, and they'll probably look here first."

"All right," Nargri said.

They went back down the stairs. When they got to the bottom, Nargri turned left into one of the side corridors. Limper followed her through a series of corridors, all more or less alike, dimly lit and silent. They moved as quietly as they could and stopped from time to time to listen for the sounds of dragons. But they heard nothing except the sounds they themselves made. At last they came to a flight of stairs and went down it. At its bottom was a stone door, which Nargri opened. They went outside, and Nargri closed the door behind them. They were at the top of a steep slope, overgrown with bushes and saplings. Limper looked around at the brown and yellow foliage. The air was damp and had an earthy smell. "This is certainly a lot better. I don't really belong underground."

"I'm not sure I do either," Nargri said. "Let's get away from the door."

They couldn't find a path, so they went down through the bushes. At the bottom of the slope there was a narrow track for horses. No cart could have gone over it. It went northwest-southeast along the edge of a tree-filled ravine. There was a river at the ravine's bottom. Limper could hear it, but he couldn't see it. He looked up and down the road, seeing nothing except weeds, then turned onto it, going northwest. He went slowly, since his bad leg was still bothering him. Nargri stayed by his side.

IN TROLL WOOD

They walked all day, stopping a couple of times, where streams crossed the road, to get a drink of water and to rest. They had nothing to eat. Nargri kept saying she was hungry. Finally Limper said, "If you say that one more time, I'll eat you."

"You've said that before."

"This time I mean it."

"All right," Nargri said. "I'll keep quiet."

By mid-afternoon Limper's bad leg was really aching, and he was certain he had a cold. The valley they were walking through widened, and the valley floor flattened. The river spread out into a long, narrow lake, full of rushes. The rushes were full of birds, and flocks of ducks floated on the open water. A little before sunset they stopped. Limper waded into the lake and caught four fish, then made a fire and cooked them. After they'd eaten, Nargri curled up next to him and went to sleep.

Limper sat looking at the fire, his back against a tree. He was almost asleep when he heard horses coming toward them. He got up. Nargri stirred and hissed softly. Limper walked to the road and waited there, in the shadow of a tree. It was twilight. He couldn't make out the horses till they were close to him. There was a rider on the first horse. The second horse was saddled and bridled, but riderless. The rider reined his horse close to where Limper stood and looked toward the fire. Nargri was still sleeping close by the fire, her tail over her nose.

"What in hell is that?" the rider said out loud. He had a boy's high voice, and he spoke the language of the northerners.

"She's a dragon," Limper said in the same language.

The rider started. His horse jerked up its head. "Where are you?" the rider asked and looked around.

Limper stepped out into the road. "If you want company, you're welcome, but I have no food and nothing worth stealing."

"That isn't much of an offer, but it isn't likely I'll get a better offer anywhere around here," the rider said. He turned his horse off the road toward the fire. Limper walked beside him. When he reached the fire, the rider dismounted and tethered his horses, then unsaddled them. The firelight lit him, so Limper could see what he looked like: a boy about fifteen, tall and thin with dark hair and dark eyes. His eyebrows came together above his nose, in a single long, thick, straight, dark line.

When the boy was done tending to his horses, he pulled a dead rabbit out of his saddlebag and came over to the fire. He sat down and started to clean the rabbit. Nargri woke and stretched, then she moved closer to where the boy sat and watched him work.

"Your dragon looks hungry," the boy said after a while.

"She is," Limper said.

"Do dragons eat rabbits? The stories I've heard about dragons didn't tell what they ate, except for people."

"There isn't that much difference between dragons and men. They both eat what they can get."

The boy finished cleaning the rabbit, then went into the wood, gathered branches, and built a spit. When the rabbit was on the spit over the fire, the boy sat down close enough to the fire so he'd be able to reach out and turn the rabbit. Limper sat down on the other side of the fire. After a while the boy looked at him and said, "I'm called Coalbrow."

Limper said, "Holrin is my name. That's Nargri watching your rabbit."

Coalbrow looked at Nargri. "This is the first time I've seen a dragon. I thought they were bigger."

"She's a child," Limper said, "and somewhat undersized for her age."

Coalbrow turned the rabbit. "I never met anyone who'd even seen a dragon before this."

"They're uncommon nowadays."

When the rabbit was done, Coalbrow shared it with them. They ate, then Nargri went back to sleep. Coalbrow looked around. "If you have a horse, it's well hidden."

Limper shook his head. "I had one a while back, but I have trouble holding onto things."

"I have a spare horse, and I'd as soon have company," Coalbrow said.

"Where are you going?" Limper asked.

"Home, to the north," Coalbrow said. "I plan to ride to Yara Shoi, then take passage on a ship."

"I've been thinking of going up north to see how my kinfolk are doing," Limper said. "And I'm getting tired of walking."

Coalbrow nodded, then settled himself to sleep. After a while Limper lay down. The night was cold. Nargri woke and came over to Limper and curled up against him. He put his arm around her.

In the morning the three of them went on. The day was cold and windy. Clouds covered most of the sky. The valley they rode through narrowed, and the lake they rode beside turned back into a river, rapid-flowing and full of stones. At sunset they saw two deer at the river's edge, drinking. The deer saw them and turned and ran, but Coalbrow had his bow in his hand; and one of the deer, a young buck, didn't get away. They ate well that evening. While they were eating Limper asked, "What part of the north do you come from?"

Coalbrow said, "I was born in the south, and my mother was a southerner, but my father was from the western firths."

"What was he doing in the south? Soldiering?"

Coalbrow nodded. "He was in the king's guard at Arinat till he got sick. He said he didn't mind working with foreigners, but he didn't want to be buried with them. So we started north. He died in the mountains. I decided to go north anyway, since I have kinfolk there whom I haven't met."

After they ate, they lay down to sleep, Limper wrapped in a cloak he'd borrowed from Coalbrow.

Nargri was curled up beside him. He felt cold and achey, and his nose was starting to get stopped up. There was no doubt now that he had a cold.

The next day was windless, misty and cold. They had venison for breakfast, saddled the horses and rode on. From time to time rain fell, so fine that Limper barely felt it. His cold was getting worse, and he didn't talk much, but did a lot of coughing and sneezing. They stopped early and made camp beside the river, among trees that had changed color and were beginning to lose their leaves. The ground was wet. Limper sat close by the fire, wrapped in Coalbrow's cloak. He wasn't hungry. He didn't eat much, and he went to sleep as soon as he'd eaten. It was still raining the next morning. The rain was so light that it didn't get through the leaves; and Limper didn't feel it till he went to the river's edge where there were no leaves. His cold was as bad as ever, and he had a headache.

They had venison for breakfast again, then saddled the horses and went on. The rain kept up all morning, soaking through the cloak Limper had on, and Limper's cold got no better.

The hills were getting lower and less steep. About noon the rain stopped, but the sky stayed low and grey. The river was rising. Where the river bank was low, the river went over it, spreading onto the road; and the horses splashed through shallow water. Late in the afternoon they came to another road that was wide and looked well-traveled. Coalbrow said, "Unless I'm lost, which is possible, this is the road to Yara Shoi."

"There's a way to find out," Limper said.

They turned onto the road, going north. It went through a wide valley, between low hills. There were places on either side of the road where the forest had been cleared to make hay fields or pastures. Here and there they saw smoke rising that must have come from some farmhouse smoke-hole. At twilight they saw a farmhouse close by the road, on top of a grassy hill. They rode up to it. Limper dismounted and knocked on the door. A man opened the door and looked at them, then said in the language of the northerners, "Trouble comes in threes. The hay's rotting in the fields, my best cow is sick, and now I have visitors."

"If you want us to go away, we will," Limper said.

"If you go, I'll be back to having two problems and wondering what the third will be. Come on in."

"I'll look after the horses," Coalbrow said. Nargri jumped down off Limper's horse and followed Limper when he went into the house.

"What's that?" the man asked, looking at her.

"A dragon," Limper said.

The man said, "I'll say one thing for living beside a main road, I get to meet all kinds of people. Sit down. I'll have my wife get you something to eat."

Limper sat down on a bench by a table, and Nargri climbed up beside him. The man went out of the room. After a moment a woman came in. She was big and fat with yellow hair, a red face and bright blue, bulging eyes. She set a plate down in front of Limper, then set a mug full of ale next to the plate. There was smoked fish on the plate, also a thick slice of rye bread and a big glob of butter. "My husband says you have a dragon," the woman said.

Limper nodded. The woman looked at Nargri.

"If that's what all the famous dragon killers were killing, I don't think much of them."

Coalbrow came in, carrying a haunch of venison. He gave it to the woman and said, "Little good is said about guests who bring only their appetites."

"That's true," the woman said. Then she got food for Coalbrow. The man came back into the room, an apple in his hand. He sat down and bit into the apple. While he was chewing, he said, "Are you going north or south?"

"North," Coalbrow said.

The woman said, "There was a fellow here a day or two back, who said there was snow in the mountains."

Coalbrow nodded. Limper said, "There is."

The man said, "If that's so, then winter's coming early, and I have almost no hay in my barn. Whatever you two do for a living, stick to it. Don't take up farming."

"I'll remember that," Limper said.

Then the man said, "If you're going north, I'd better tell you what lies in that direction. A day's ride from here, there's a part of the forest that's called Troll Wood. Some people say trolls live there. I don't think that's any too likely, but, from what I've heard, a lot of travelers have trouble getting through the wood, especially those who travel alone or with only one or two companions."

"How will we know when we've gotten to Troll Wood?" Coalbrow asked.

The man said, "People tell me that the folk who live in the wood put animal skulls in trees to mark the boundaries of their country. When you see one of those markers, be careful."

"Do you know anything about the people in the wood?" Limper asked.

The man shook his head. "All I've heard about them is, they're unfriendly and unpeaceful and very hairy."

After that they lay down close by the fire and went to sleep. In the morning the woman of the house made breakfast for them. After they ate they went out and saddled their horses. The woman came out and gave Limper a loaf of rye bread and some apples. "No one should travel without food."

Limper took the food and put it in a saddlebag. "Thank you."

They told the woman farewell, then they went on. The sky was overcast, and the air was damp. From time to time a fine rain fell. Still it seemed to Limper that his cold was getting a little better. The land flattened out, and after a while he saw no more signs of people anywhere around. Weeds grew across the road. Alongside it there were bushes and saplings. A little way back from it there were huge trees, their leaves brown or yellow. Late in the afternoon Coalbrow said, "Look," and pointed. There was a bear skull stuck in the crotch of a tree a little way off the road.

"We'd better make camp here," he said. "If what that fellow said was true, I don't want to be caught in Troll Wood at night."

"I'm not going to spend the night underneath that thing," Limper said. "Let's go back a ways."

Coalbrow nodded. They turned their horses and went back the way they'd come. After they'd gone a couple of miles Coalbrow stopped his horse. Limper heard the sound of running water off to one side. "Is this far enough?" Coalbrow asked. Limper nodded. They turned off the road. It was dark under the trees. When they got to the stream, Limper looked back. The road was out of sight, hidden by the bushes that grew along it. They dismounted and let their horses drink, then drank themselves. Then Limper said, "It seems to me we'd better camp by the road. The horses will be able to find food there."

"All right," Coalbrow said.

They led their horses back to the road and tethered them in the weeds, then unsaddled them. After that they looked for wood. Most of what they found was damp, and they had trouble getting a fire going. When it did get going, it gave off a lot of smoke and not much heat. They ate the food the farmwife had given them, then Coalbrow unpacked a needle and thread and mended a tear in his cloak. A wind started to blow that made the bushes and saplings sway and rustle. Coalbrow finished mending his cloak and put the needle and thread away, then wrapped the cloak around him and lay down to sleep. Limper sat up a while longer. When he began to feel sleepy, he shook Nargri till she woke. "What is it?" she asked.

"Keep watch a while. This forest makes me uneasy."

"All right," she said.

Limper lay down and went to sleep. He woke some time later. It was still dark. The fire was out, and Nargri was asleep. He sat up and stayed awake till morning. The sky cleared before sunrise; the day was bright and cold; and his cold was going away. They ate what was left of the venison, then went on. The road led into low hills, full of gullies and outcroppings of rock. In one place a spring came up out of the rocks beside the road. Seven or eight poles had been wedged between rocks around the spring. There were deer skulls stuck on top of the poles. Most of the skulls still had their horns, and the horns had been painted red.

A little way beyond the spring, the road went into a narrow, twisting valley. On one side of them was a steep slope covered with stones, with brown-leafed bushes growing here and there between the stones. On the other side was a river, brimfull of water. The water was moving quickly, swirling around boulders and sliding down over small drops. Across the river there was another steep slope covered with stones. When they had been traveling through the valley for some time, Limper heard a rumbling sound, looked up and saw rocks tumbling down the hillside toward them. He yelled, "Look out," and yanked his horse around, kicking the horse's sides. The horse ran; and he grabbed onto Nargri with his free hand to keep her from falling. He looked back. Coalbrow had turned his horse and was coming after him. A rock as big as a man's head hit the road behind him and ahead of Coalbrow. Limper looked ahead along the road they had already traveled. Some distance in front of him he saw men, five or six of them, standing in the road. They were armed with spears. He heard Coalbrow's horse neigh and looked back again. The horse had stopped. Limper looked up the hill. The landslide seemed over. He reined his horse and shouted, "What's wrong?"

"A stone hit him," Coalbrow said and dismounted.

Limper turned his horse and went back. Coalbrow had crouched and was looking at the horse's right foreleg. He felt along the leg. The horse started back. Coalbrow let go and waited till Limper reached him, then said, "Hold him, will you."

Limper looked back. The men in the road hadn't

moved. He dismounted and took hold of the horse's bridle, telling the horse in a soothing voice, "There, there, you idiot. This is for your own good."

Coalbrow felt along the leg again, then stood. "There's a little blood, but I can't feel any break in the bone." He took hold of the horse's bridle. Limper let go.

Nargri said, "Those men are coming toward us, Limper."

"I can see that."

Coalbrow led his horse a few steps. The horse was limping badly. Coalbrow had to pull hard to get the horse moving, and keep tugging to keep him moving. He stopped finally and looked down the road. "Do those fellows look friendly to you, Holrin?"

Limper shook his head, then looked the way they'd been going before the landslide hit. Rocks and gravel covered the road now, but it didn't look as if they'd be difficult to get over. "We'd better leave your horse here and go on as best we can."

Coalbrow shrugged. "All right." He got his bow and quiver, then Limper mounted and pulled him up behind him, and they went on. They had to dismount when they reached the place where the landslide covered the road. Limper led the horse over the rubble. Nargri, who stayed crouched on the saddle, her claws dug into the leather, said, "Those men are getting close, and they don't look like other men. I think they must be trolls."

Limper sighed. When they'd crossed the rubble, he mounted and Coalbrow mounted behind him. They went on. A moment or two later, they heard a scream behind them, and they looked back. It was Coalbrow's horse that had screamed. The horse was on his knees, the men around him, their spears in him. As they looked, the horse fell over. Limper slapped his horse with the reins, and the horse went on more quickly.

After a moment Coalbrow said, "That was a foolish thing for them to do. My horse was a good horse."

Limper shrugged.

They kept going, and the men kept following them, keeping pretty far back. The valley narrowed, and the valley sides grew steeper. The river narrowed too, and ran faster, foaming white where it went around boulders. Coalbrow said, "This place looks as if it could be turned into a good trap."

"I was thinking of that myself," Limper said.

Shortly after that they saw men ahead, six of them, standing in the road, waiting. Limper stopped his horse. He looked at the hillside and said, "We'll never get the horse up that. Anyway, I think somebody started that landslide. There may well be people up there." Then he looked at the river. There were no rocks to be seen in this section of it. The current was moving quickly, but the river's surface was smooth. "Can you swim, Coalbrow?"

"No."

"I can, a little," Nargri said.

Limper said, "You go up the hill, Nargri. You're small and can hide, and they're not likely to bother with you."

"I don't like leaving you when you're in trouble."

"I'm not doing it for your good. If we can't get out of this, you'll be free to rescue us."

"That makes sense," Nargri said. She jumped

down off the horse and scurried up the hillside, hurrying from one rock to the next.

Limper dismounted. "I think we'll do better in the river than on dry land. Come on." He unbuckled his sword belt, took it off, then rebuckled it and hooked it over the saddlehorn.

"I hope you know what you're doing." Coalbrow dismounted also.

They led the horse to the water. He balked, and they had to tug at the reins to get him to go in. By this time the men, both those before and those behind them, were running toward them. Limper waded into the water, pulling on the horse's reins to make him follow. "Get ahold of the saddlehorn and keep ahold of it."

The water was cold and fast moving, even close to the bank. He was soon thigh deep in it and then waist deep, then deeper. The horse began swimming, and Limper grabbed ahold of the saddle. Coalbrow was on the other side of the horse, holding onto the saddlehorn with one hand, his other hand wound in the horse's mane. He was frowning, and his face was paler than usual. Limper looked back at the shore. The men had stopped on the bank and were standing watching them, as the current carried them downriver.

By this time the horse was about a third of the way across the river. It seemed to Limper that the current was quickening. Ahead he saw boulders in the river. He swore aloud. After a moment he said, "The horse ought to do better if he's dragging only one of us instead of two." He let go of the saddle and started swimming. The horse was upriver from him and broke the force of the current somewhat. At first he was able to keep beside the horse. But it was soon evident that the horse was a better swim-

mer than he was. Soon he was behind the horse
and feeling the full force of the current. It carried
him downriver, away from the horse. By this time
they were two-thirds of the way across the river
and well below the point where they'd entered the
water, almost to the boulders. The current was
much quicker now. It swirled him against a boulder, and he grabbed at it, but he couldn't keep
hold of the smooth, slippery surface. A moment or
two later the current carried him further down the
river and tumbled him over a drop. For a moment
he was underwater, his mouth full of water, so he
was choking. Then he got his head above water,
and he coughed and spat. He glanced back and
saw the horse no longer swimming, but standing,
his head down, knee deep in water, Coalbrow
beside him, looking downriver. Then the current
spun him around, and he saw more boulders
ahead, the water foaming white around them. The
valley was narrowing again, and on his side of the
river, the valley wall turned into a cliff, rising
straight up out of the water. He went over another
drop and went underwater again, one foot touching
the river bottom. He pushed himself up, getting
his head back above water. The current brought
him against another boulder, and he hit his shoulder. The water was white all around him. The river
went down over another small drop. He was getting tired, and his shoulder hurt, and he was having trouble keeping his head above water. But the
water was becoming less turbulent. The current
brought him close to a boulder. He grabbed it and
held on. For a while he did nothing except hold
on, his arms wrapped around the boulder, as he
gasped for breath. Then he lifted his head and
looked around. The river had spread out again. In

front of him it was smooth, its surface unbroken by boulders. The bank nearest him was still sheer and bare, rising straight out of the river. He looked to the far side of the river. The bank there was low and sloped gently up from the water.

He stayed where he was, holding onto the rock, till he was breathing slowly and easily. By that time both his arms ached. At last ne said out loud, "It seems to me most people manage to stay out of situations like this. I must be either unlucky or stupid." Then he let go of the rock and started to swim toward the river's far shore. The current was still fast, and it was hard work swimming across it. A short time after he let go of the rock, he was a good distance downriver from it, but the far shore seemed to be getting no closer. He swam slowly and evenly with deep strokes, though what he wanted to do was move his arms and legs as quickly as he was able. After a while he saw that the shore was closer than it had been. He was beginning to gasp for breath, and it was getting more and more difficult to move his arms and legs. Then one of his feet touched bottom. He stopped swimming, stood and waded the rest of the way to shore. He sat down on the rocky bank, so tired that he was shaking. His heart was beating hard, and his throat and lungs hurt. He stayed still a long time, his head down, his eyes shut, listening to the sound of his heart beating and the sound of the river. At last he began to notice that he was wet and cold, and that the shoulder he'd hit was aching. He opened his eyes and looked around. The road was behind him, ten or fifteen feet away. Beyond it was a steep, rocky hillside, bare except for a few brown bushes. There was nothing in sight except the river and the bare slopes and the road. By this time, he'd stopped shaking and started shivering. His teeth were chattering. He pushed his wet hair back out of his eyes and stood up and stumbled to the road. There was no one in sight on it, either before or behind. After a moment he shrugged, which made his shoulder hurt more than before, then grimaced, then said aloud, "I'll only get colder sitting still." He started along the road in the same direction they'd been going, before they'd met up with the hairy men. He was still tired. After he'd gone a little way, he sat down at the side of the road and rested. When he got up and looked down the road, he saw the men, way behind him and coming toward him. He looked at them a moment, then said, "May they get all the worst diseases." After that he started to climb the hillside. It was steep with lots of loose gravel on it, so he kept slipping back and sending stones rattling down the hill behind him. By the time he was halfway up the hill, the first of the men were below him, pointing at him and shouting. Limper kept climbing. The men started up the hill after him. They were better climbers than he was and moved quickly up over the stones with only a few slips. He stopped looking back; it took too much time; but he could hear them shouting to one another as they climbed. After a while he realized he could understand them. They were speaking the language of the dragons.

"We have him this time," one called.

"You said that last time," another one said.

"Where's his big knife?" a third one shouted. "I can't see it."

"If he had one, he'd probably cut you with it," a fourth man said.

"But I wanted a big knife," the third man said.

By this time the voices sounded close behind him, and the top of the hill was still a long way off. Limper grabbed a big stone and turned to face the men. They stopped. This was the first time he'd been close enough to the men to get a good look at them. They looked more or less like other men, except that they were covered with hair from head to foot. They had thick ridges above their eyes, short foreheads and huge jaws. They wore kilts made out of animal skins and hats made out of pelts of the heads of wolves, except for one, whose hat was made from the head of a bear. All of them carried little round shields, covered with some kind of hide, and five of them had spears that were long poles, sharpened at one end. The sixth had a sword, its blade red with rust from point to guard.

One of them started to move. Limper said in the language of the dragons, "Stay put, or I'll do my best to bash your head in."

The hairy man with the bear hat said, "Why do you speak our language?"

"It would be foolish to speak to you in a language you didn't understand."

"But none of the other unmen spoke our language," the hairy man said.

"Let's not fritter away the whole day," the hairy man who had the sword said. "I have other things I want to do." He took a step toward Limper, and Limper lifted the rock and got ready to heave it.

"You always want to strike before you think, Atsif," a third hairy man said.

The hairy man called Atsif stopped. "What do you mean by that, Utlex?"

"I have a new son, who needs a name. Since this fellow speaks our language, I can ask him his name and use it for my son."

The hairy man with the bear hat nodded. "That sounds like a good idea. An unman's name ought to be lucky, since the unmen have many wonderful things that we men lack."

The other hairy men nodded, except for Atsif, who shrugged. "All right, but be quick about it."

"What's your name?" Utlex asked Limper.

After a moment Limper said, "First, tell me what ceremonies you people go through, when you name a son."

"We do what all men do," Utlex said. "The father goes out and kills a man and cooks the man's brain with herbs and eats it. Then he gives the man's name to his son."

Limper shook his head. "I want no part of that ceremony."

"At this rate, it'll be dark before we get home," Atsif said. He started toward Limper.

"No," Utlex shouted, but Atsif was almost to Limper. Limper threw the rock as hard as he was able. It hit the top rim of Atsif's shield and bounced against Atsif's cheek. Atsif grunted and staggered. Limper stepped toward him, grabbing ahold of his sword hand and twisting it. But Atsif didn't let go of the sword. Instead he kicked Limper's bad leg, and Limper almost fell. Then Limper felt another one of the hairy men grab his right arm. He shoved his elbow into the man's gut. The man said, "Huh," and let go of him. At the same moment Atsif yanked his hand free of Limper's grip and jabbed at him with the sword. Limper stepped back. The sword's point came close, but didn't touch him. A couple more of the hairy men grabbed onto his arms. He tried to twist free and felt a sharp pain in the shoulder he'd hit. The hairy men kept hold of him. Atsif stepped toward Limper. Utlex stepped in between. "Not yet, Atsif. I want this fellow's name."

Atsif stopped. "Once you get hold of an idea, you never let go."

Utlex turned toward Limper. "Now, tell me your name."

"I don't see why I should. Why should I care whether or not your son gets a name?"

"If you don't tell me, I'll torture you till you do."

"If you hurt me, I'll make up a name. What'll happen to your son, if he has a name that isn't a real name?"

Utlex frowned. Another one of the hairy men said, "It seems to me your son would die, Utlex. How could he be a real person, if his name wasn't a real name?"

"Discussions about religion make my head ache," Atsif said. "Let's kill him and get on home."

"Anything worth having is worth going to an effort to get," Limper said. "It seems to me, Utlex, you ought to be able to figure out a way to make me tell you my real name."

Utlex kept on frowning. Finally he said, "I don't see how."

"I think I know how," the man with the bear hat said. "The sorcerer knows spells that only work if he knows the name of the person he's putting the spell on. If we take this fellow to the sorcerer and torture him till he tells us a name, then the sorcerer can use whatever name he tells us in a spell. If the spell works, we will know the name is his real name."

"What will we do, if the spell doesn't work?"

"Torture him some more, till he tells us another name. Sooner or later, he'll have to tell us his real name."

The other hairy men nodded. One of them said, "That's a good idea, Ko."

Utlex grinned. His teeth were yellow, and a lot of them were broken. Atsif grunted and shrugged. "I can see we aren't going to get home tonight. We'll be lucky to get this over with before tomorrow morning."

The two hairy men who were holding Limper pushed him forward. He stumbled and slipped down the hill, the hairy men going with him, keeping hold of him. When they reached the hill's bottom, one of the hairy men holding him said, "Are we going to have to keep hold of him all the way to the sorcerer's cave?"

The hairy man named Ko shook his head. "He won't be able to run away from us. His leg is lame. Let him go."

The men let go of Limper, and he rubbed first one arm and then the other. Then they set off along the road, the same way Limper had been going before he met them. There were two of them in front of him and two behind and one on each side. All of them kept their weapons ready to use. They went quickly, so that Limper had trouble keeping up. Atsif was behind him and kept pushing him ahead. At last Atsif said, "If you give your son this fellow's name, Utlex, he'll be always falling behind."

"That may be," Utlex said. "We've noticed before that the unmen aren't as strong as we are or as quick, but still there are more and more of them, and fewer and fewer of us."

They stayed on the road till they were out of the valley, then they left it for a little side trail that wound through a wood of stunted, brown-leafed trees. Limper's bad leg began to bother him, and he had more and more trouble keeping up. Atsif pushed him more often and harder, till finally he stumbled and fell on his hands and knees. He stood up slowly, brushing the dirt and wet leaves off his pants.

"Come on. Hurry up," Atsif said.

"If you're in such a hurry to go home, why don't you go right now?" Limper asked. "I could do without your company."

Atsif shook his head.

"Don't you think they can do what they set out to do without you along?" Limper suggested.

"No," Atsif said.

The other hairy men frowned, and Ko said, "Let's find out, Atsif. You go home, and we'll take this fellow to the sorcerer and see if we can get his name by ourselves, without you."

The other hairy men nodded. Atsif shrugged. "All right, but you'll be sorry." Then he turned and went back the way they'd come.

Ko said, "Let's get going."

"You may want to get this over with, but I don't," Limper said. "My leg's hurting me. Let me rest a while."

Ko frowned. Limper said, "If you keep pushing me, I might get angry, which will make it more difficult for you to make me talk. Angry people can be very stubborn, even when somebody's hurting them."

"He's right about that," one of the other hairy men said. "When my wife gets mad at me, she stops talking, and there's nothing I can do to her to make her say a word, until she's over her anger. Then when she starts talking, I'm sorry she did."

The hairy men all grinned and nodded. Ko said, "All right, unman. We'll let you rest."

"Thank you," Limper said. He sat down on a rock outcropping, stretching his bad leg out in front of him. The hairy men stood leaning on their spears. After a while Limper said, "One thing I don't understand is why all of you are helping Utlex. He's going to get a name for his son, or so he thinks. But what are the rest of you going to get out of killing me?"

Ko said, "If we help Utlex get a name for his son, then he'll help us, when we have to go and get names for our sons."

"But what if you have no more sons, or what if Utlex dies before your sons are born? It seems to me, it'd be better for you to get what you can now."

Utlex frowned. "This unman talks too much."

"If you know a way we can get something out of you, except for your name, we'd like to hear about it," Ko said.

"My companion had my big knife and a knife of his own, also my shield that's made of metal, so nothing can pierce it. If you return me to him alive, he'll give you all these things."

The hairy men grinned, and Ko shook his head. "Can't you count, unman? Six of us went down along the river to see what'd happened to you, but there were six more of us; and they stayed to look after your companion. He won't get away from them."

"I hope you're wrong about that," Limper said.

"We've rested long enough," Ko said. "Come on, unman."

Limper sighed and stood up, and they went on. His bad leg still gave him trouble. He went slowly, and his limp grew worse and worse.

"Atsif may well be right," one of the hairy men

said. "If you give your son this fellow's name, he's likely to be lame, and what use is a lame man?"

Limper's face turned red, but he said nothing. Utlex shrugged. Ko said, "Who's ever been able to talk Utlex out of anything, once he decided to do it?"

The trail they followed went out of the wood and into a series of narrow gorges. The ground became stonier, and the trees covering the hillsides were scrawny-looking pines. There was more and more bare rock. Finally the trail entered a valley, full of bushes and stunted oak trees. The valley walls were bare stone, and the trail went beside a shallow stream, full of rocks. After a while the valley narrowed, and the stream filled most of it. The trail went along a stone ledge, maybe ten feet wide, between the stream and the valley wall. There were red handprints on the rock walls, some of them so faded that Limper had trouble making them out, others bright red. The ledge narrowed till it was three or four feet wide. They walked single file, first Utlex, then Ko, then Limper, then the rest. By this time it was late afternoon. The sky was still bright blue, but the valley was entirely in shadow. The further they went into the valley, the more red handprints there were on the walls. The stream was running fast, white with foam, and the valley was full of the sound of it. The ledge got even narrower, till there was barely room on it for them to walk. By this time there was nothing around them except bare stone, and a few weeds that grew out of cracks in the stone. Ahead of them the valley ended, and there was a wall of rock, a waterfall spilling down it.

Limper said, "I can't say I like being in this place."

"That's because it's holy," Ko said. "One way you can tell a place is holy, is that you feel uneasy there."

After a moment Limper said, "It's certainly true that I always feel uncomfortable in temples."

"What else can you expect? Holy places are full of spirits, and spirits and men have never gotten on well. It seems, from what you say, that spirits don't get on well with unmen, either. Only a man who has a lot of magic, such as our sorcerer, can stay in a place like this that's full of spirits."

The valley widened before it came to an end, and there was a pool below the waterfall, shallow and full of big boulders. The trail went around one side of the pool. They followed it. Limper's clothes were almost dry by now, but the spray from the waterfall got them wet again. The trail went all the way to the waterfall. When they reached its end, Ko and Utlex went in behind the waterfall. The man behind Limper shoved him forward, and he followed them, going slowly and keeping close to the cliff. Spray drenched him. He could hear nothing except the sound of water. It fell only a foot or two in front of him, a grey, shimmering wall. After he'd gone maybe ten feet, he came to a shallow cave, dimly lit by the light that came through the waterfall. Ko and Utlex waited there. Limper stopped and looked around. The cave's walls were covered with water. Here and there on them were red handprints, their edges blurred where the paint had spread. At the back of the cave was an opening. Ko grabbed hold of him and pushed him toward the opening. He went in, the others following him. Ahead of them was a long tunnel, at the end of which a fire burned.

Ko pushed him again, and he went on. After

they'd gone halfway down the tunnel, Ko and Utlex stopped. Ko called, "Sorcerer! Can we come
in?"

Then something stepped into the tunnel ahead
of them. It was lit from behind by the firelight, and
it looked more or less like a man, except that its
head was perfectly round and had horns like deerhorns coming out of it. A bushy tail hung down between its legs, and it had shaggy forearms and
paws instead of hands. In one paw, it held an ax.
"Who is it?" the thing called. It had a deep,
muffled voice.

"Ko and Utlex and three others. We have an unman with us."

"What do you want?" the thing asked.

"Utlex wants the unman's name for his son, but
the unman won't tell us what his name is. We
thought you could help us find it out."

"I'll pay you, sorcerer," Utlex said.

"What?"

"The next deer I kill, also a dressed deerskin,
also one of my wife's bark baskets."

"That's not enough," the thing said. "I want two
of your wife's baskets, both of them full of food
she's gathered."

Utlex sighed. "All right."

"Come in, then," the thing said.

They went the rest of the way down the tunnel.
When they got close to the thing, Limper saw that
it was a man, dressed up in animal skins and wearing a mask with deerhorns attached to it. The mask
was as round and white as a full moon and flat and
blank except for two eyeholes. The sorcerer
stepped aside. They went past him into a second
cave. This one was long and low, its walls and
floors and ceiling all painted red. A small fire at the

tunnel's entrance lit the front of the cave. The back of the cave was out of sight in darkness. On the floor beyond the fire was a man's skull in the center of a circle of stones. The skull had thick brow-ridges, so it seemed likely to Limper that it was the skull of a hairy man. One of its temples was crushed in, as if it had been hit a hard blow there. Limper looked around at the ax the sorcerer held. The ax head was made of stone that had been chipped into shape. It was big and thick and looked heavy. The sorcerer turned his head, so his white mask was facing Limper, and Limper saw eyes glinting behind the mask's eyeholes.

Ko cleared his throat. "We planned to torture the unman till he told us his name, but he said he'd make up a name. We thought if we brought him to you, you could use whatever name he told us in a spell, and if the spell worked, we'd know the name was his name. If the spell didn't work, we'd torture him some more."

The sorcerer kept looking at Limper, saying nothing.

Utlex coughed, then scratched his head. "Well, sorcerer?"

"That would take a long time. It seems to me it would better if I put a spell on him, so he won't be able to lie. That will take less time."

The hairy men nodded. Utlex said, "That's a better idea than Ko's."

"I'm not going to make my magic with a lot of people watching."

Ko said, "We'll wait outside."

One of the hairy men pushed Limper toward the tunnel.

"Leave the unman here," the sorcerer said. "I can't put a spell on him if he's not present."

"But that's not safe," Utlex said. "What if he tries to get away?"

"I'll get some rope, and you can tie him up before you leave," the sorcerer said.

The hairy men nodded. The sorcerer went into the darkness at the back of the cave and returned with a rawhide rope. He gave the rope to Ko. Ko tied Limper's hands behind his back, then said, "I'll need some more rope to tie his feet, sorcerer."

"I saw him coming down the tunnel," the sorcerer said. "He can barely walk as it is. There's no need to tie his feet. Anyway, I don't have any more rope."

Ko frowned, but the other hairy men nodded, and Utlex said, "The sorcerer is right." He looked at Limper. "There's only one way out of this cave, unman, and that's this tunnel, and we'll be at the other end of it." Then he went out of the cave into the tunnel, the other men following him. Ko left last, looking back at Limper and frowning.

When the hairy men were gone, the sorcerer went into the back of the cave and got some flat stones, which he put on the fire. Then he set a basket beside the fire. Its outside was covered with something that looked like tar. Beside the basket he put a hide bag that seemed to be full of some liquid, and a couple of little leather pouches that had clusters of brown and white bird feathers attached to them. Limper watched the sorcerer and twisted his hands, testing the rope that tied him. It was tightly wrapped around his wrists. The knot in it didn't slip at all. "Do you think you can make me tell my name?"

The sorcerer stopped and turned his masked face toward him. "I don't see why not. I have the help of the spirits that inhabit this valley, and I know how to make a drink that makes men so drunk that they see things they don't usually see, such as ghosts and monsters. When a person is that drunk, he's likely to say things he meant to keep to himself."

"What if I won't drink this drink of yours?"

"We'll get it into you one way or another, and if you end up with fewer teeth than you had before, I'm sure Utlex won't mind."

Limper tried to tug his hands apart. The knot still held. "Is there no way I can get out of this alive?"

The sorcerer shook his head.

"I'll give Utlex my name to give to his son. He doesn't have to kill me to get it. I don't use it much anyway."

"Don't you know a man can't give his name away? It's his till he dies."

"But I'm not a man. I'm an unman. That's what you keep calling me."

"That makes no difference," the sorcerer said.

"Ko and his friends didn't think to search me. They were too busy worrying about how to get my name to wonder what else I might have."

"Ah?" the sorcerer said.

"I have a necklace around my neck that's made of gold. I'll give it to you, if you'll untie my hands."

The sorcerer laughed. "How can you stop me from taking it with your hands tied?"

"I can't, but when Ko and Utlex and the rest come back, I'll tell them about the necklace. Do you think they'll let you keep it?"

"Then I'll kill you before they come back," the sorcerer said. "Dead folk have little to say for themselves."

Limper grinned. "How will Utlex feel if you kill me before he gets my name to give his son?"

The sorcerer grunted, then went over to the fire, lifted his mask and spat on one of the stones he'd set there. The stone was still cold, and the sorcerer's spittle didn't start to sizzle. He opened the hide bag and poured water from it into the basket, then closed the bag and set it down. "I don't even know that you have a necklace."

"I can't take it out and show it to you. My hands are tied."

The sorcerer stood still, his mask turned toward Limper, then at last he said, "If you try anything, I'll give you a good whack with my ax, and not the flat side of it, either."

"My hands are tied, and I've got one lame leg. I'd be hard put to harm a child."

"All I know is that you talk too much, and I get dizzy listening to you. No one who can do that to me is entirely harmless."

Limper shrugged. His shoulder still hurt. "Well, if you don't want the necklace, that's your choice."

The sorcerer tightened his grip on the ax and came over. When he got close, Limper could smell him. He stank of sweat and some kind of animal grease. From the look of his bare chest, he was middle-aged. His flesh was beginning to sag and wrinkle. The matted hair that covered him was going grey. He fumbled one-handed till he got hold of the necklace, then pulled it up over Limper's head. It caught on one of Limper's ears. Limper said, "Careful," but the sorcerer kept pulling, and after a moment, the necklace came free.

"Is my ear still on?"

The sorcerer grunted, looking at the necklace dangling from his hand. It was the one Limper had taken from Gatix's house, the links made of red gold, shaped into flowers. The gold glinted in the firelight. The hand that held it was big and hairy and dirty with badly bitten fingernails. At last the sorcerer lifted his head, so Limper was looking at the blank, white mask. "All right, unman. I'll untie you. I can say Ko tied you badly, and it's his fault that you got away." He tucked the necklace out of sight in his kilt, then tucked his ax under one arm and went around behind Limper. After a moment Limper felt him fumbling at the rope. The rope was well tied. It took some time to undo the knots. At last the rope loosened, and Limper pulled his hands free, then turned so he could see the sorcerer. The sorcerer said. "You'd better go out the back way."

Limper rubbed his wrists. "Where—"

Up in the tunnel, people started shouting. Nargri shrieked, "Limper, Limper, where are you?"

The sorcerer grabbed at his ax, which was still under his arm. Limper punched him in the gut as hard as he could. The sorcerer grunted and clutched his belly with both hands, his ax dropping from under his arm. Limper shoved him backward. He stumbled, almost falling. Limper grabbed up the ax, shouting, "In here, Nargri."

The sorcerer straightened up and started toward Limper. Limper swung the ax up. "Stop that."

The sorcerer stopped. Limper stepped back. "Think about the necklace of gold. You want to keep it, don't you?"

"One thing is certain, unman. I don't want that ax in me."

There was a scurrying sound in the tunnel. "Nargri?" Limper called. "Is that you?"

"Limper, hurry. Coalbrow's in trouble."

"You go ahead of me," Limper said to the sorcerer. "And remember that I have the ax."

The sorcerer started toward the tunnel, and Limper followed him. Nargri came running out of the tunnel, stopping when she saw Limper. On her side there was an area where dark blood covered her glistening scales, and Limper could see drops of blood on the cave floor behind her.

"Come on," she said to Limper. She turned and started back into the tunnel.

"Stop where you are, Nargri." Limper grabbed onto one of the sorcerer's arms and pulled him to a stop. "How badly are you hurt?"

"I'm not hurt," Nargri said. "Limper, Coalbrow is in trouble."

"To hell with Coalbrow. Come here."

"No," Nargri said and ran into the tunnel.

Limper yelled, "Stop," but Nargri kept on.

"What was that?" the sorcerer asked.

"Get going." Limper pushed him forward.

They went into the tunnel. At first there was enough light from the fire behind them so Limper could see where they were going. Then the tunnel grew dark, and he grabbed ahold of the sorcerer's arm. Whoever had been shouting stopped, and he heard no sound except falling water. Far ahead he saw a little dim light, where the tunnel came to an end at the cave behind the waterfall. When they got closer to the light, he saw dark shapes moving at the edges of the area of light. Suddenly the sorcerer twisted free and ran up the tunnel. Limper cursed, then followed as fast as he was able. He could see the sorcerer's dark shape ahead of him. He stumbled over something. Nargri said, "Watch it."

"Are you all right?"

"I was fine till you stepped on me. Coalbrow's outside in the cave behind the falls. Those are the trolls ahead of us."

"All right," Limper said and went on. By this time the sorcerer was almost to the tunnel's end. A dark shape moved out from the side of the tunnel, and the sorcerer screamed, so loudly that Limper could hear him through the sound of the waterfall. Then he fell. The dark shape bent over the sorcerer, then straightened up and began waving an arm. Two other dark shapes moved away from the tunnel's sides. By now Limper was close enough to the shapes so that they began to look like men. He could see Nargri too, in the dim, grey light. She was right in front of him, hurrying up the tunnel, looking back from time to time to make sure he was following. He quickened his pace. Ahead of him the three hairy men gathered around the fallen sorcerer. The sound of the water was so loud they couldn't hear Limper coming, and he was almost up to them, before one of them looked up and shouted. Nargri leaped onto the bare leg of the one who'd shouted, and he screamed and beat at her with his shield. Limper got to the hairy man nearest him before the man had time to turn around, and pushed him forward as hard as he could. The man fell into the third hairy man, who stumbled backward till he hit the tunnel wall. The first hairy man was still beating at Nargri. Limper grabbed his shield arm and shouted, "Nargri, get out."

Nargri dropped to the floor and ran. Limper pushed the hairy man forward. He staggered, almost falling. The other two hairy men started toward Limper. He hurled the ax at the first of them, and both of them ducked down behind their shields. He didn't wait to see whether the ax hit. The end of the tunnel was only a few steps away. He got to it and out into the cave, then to one side of the tunnel entrance, against the wet cave wall. There was a hairy man lying close by, his bare chest covered with blood, an arrow sticking out of his throat. It was Utlex. A few feet further on was Coalbrow, astride the horse Limper had been riding before, his bow in his hand. His pants leg was torn open midway down his thigh and soaked with blood below the tear. A bloody spear lay on the cave floor between him and Utlex. His shoulders were sagging and his head sunk forward so his chin was on his chest.

Limper hurried forward and picked up the spear, then got back to where he'd been before, beside the tunnel entrance. Nargri ran to Coalbrow's horse and shouted, "Coalbrow, it's Limper."

Slowly Coalbrow raised his head and turned it so he was looking at Limper. After a moment he said, "Are you all right?" He didn't speak loudly. Limper saw him speak more than heard him. He nodded.

"Then you take care of the rest of this," Coalbrow said. "I'm no longer able to." After he spoke, his bow dropped from his hand, and he slumped against the horse's neck. The horse moved uneasily.

"Limper," Nargri cried. "Do something."

"Are there any more hairy men outside the cave?" Limper asked, shouting.

"One. But he ran off."

"Watch the tunnel. Shout if they follow." He picked up Coalbrow's bow and hung it over the saddle horn, then gathered the horse's reins and led it out of the cave, looking back several times to

make sure Coalbrow hadn't fallen off. The horse
kept turning his head from side to side. Every time
he did that, the wet reins were almost pulled from
Limper's hands. Once again spray drenched him.
Just as they got out from behind the waterfall,
Coalbrow started to fall. Limper dropped the
spear, reached up and grabbed his sleeve, and
pulled him upright. The boy's face was greyish-
white and wet with spray. Limper looked around
quickly and saw no one near. He pulled
Coalbrow's foot out of the stirrup, still holding the
boy's sleeve with one hand, and waited for Nargri.
After a moment she came running out. Limper
grabbed her up and set her in front of Coalbrow,
more or less on top of the saddle horn, then
mounted behind Coalbrow and kicked the horse.
The horse started into a trot, and Limper put an
arm around Coalbrow's chest. He could feel Coalbrow's breasts then. They were small, but they
clearly belonged to a woman. "Well, that's a sur-
prise," he said out loud. He kicked the horse
again, and the horse began to canter. Nargri yelped
and dug her claws into the saddle horn.

They went along the trail out of the valley.
Limper kept looking back, but he didn't see the
hairy men come out of the cave. When the trail
narrowed, he reined the horse to a walk. When it
widened again, he kicked the horse into a canter.
It was close to sunset. The sky had the rich blue
color it got late in the day, and the valley shadows
were darkening. High on one wall a rock pinnacle
was in sunlight, shining yellow-white. When they
were almost out of the valley, he saw a man ahead
of them. The man turned and looked at them, then
scrambled down off the trail into the river and
crouched in the water behind a boulder. They

passed him, and Limper looked down at him. It was Ko.

A few moments later, and they were out of the valley. Limper let the horse go back to a trot. Nargri had her forefeet around the saddlehorn, her claws digging into it, and her hind feet on Coalbrow's legs, her claws digging into Coalbrow's pants. "How are you?" Limper asked.

"I'm still on this horse, which is more than I expected."

Limper touched her side, where it was bloody. "What about that?"

Nargri twisted her head back, then said, "Oh. I didn't notice that. It doesn't hurt."

"It probably will. Did you know Coalbrow was a woman?"

"Yes," Nargri said. "She was less careful around me than around you, since she thought I was an animal, at least at first."

"Why didn't you tell me?"

"It didn't seem to me it was any of your business. If you give Coalbrow any trouble, I'll start telling everyone we meet that the king of Eshgorin is offering money for you."

"What are you expecting me to do?"

"I'm not entirely sure. But my mother told me males are a strange lot and not always reliable, especially when they're around females."

Limper grinned. "I'm not going to argue with the wisdom of mothers."

They went back along the trail till they came to a spot where a rivulet tumbled down a rocky hill and across the trail. Limper reined the horse and looked around. He saw no sign of any hairy men. "You keep an eye out, Nargri." He dismounted and lifted Coalbrow down, carrying her to the rivulet. She was wearing his sword. The scabbard kept knocking against his legs. He laid her down, then looked at the wound in her thigh. By this time it had stopped bleeding, but Coalbrow had lost enough blood to dye almost all that pants leg a darker color, and the wound itself was hidden by clotted blood. He pulled off his shirt and tore a strip off the bottom, dipped it in the rivulet, then used it to wipe the blood away from the wound. When he did that, the wound began to bleed again, but very slowly. It was a gash, not a hole, not deep but long. He tore another two strips off his shirt and used them to bind the wound. When he was done, he looked at Coalbrow's face and saw that her eyes were open. "Do you think you have enough shirt left to make it worth wearing?"

"I'm not sure."

She started to get up. Limper said, "Stay still while I have a look at Nargri. After that we'll get going."

She lay back down. Limper stood up, went to the horse and picked up Nargri.

"What're you doing?" she asked.

"I'm going to take a look at your side. That blood must've come from somewhere."

"It's only a scratch."

"That may well be." He set Nargri down beside the rivulet and scooped up some water and splashed it on her.

"Ai! That's cold, Limper."

He used his shirt to wipe her off, then looked her over. There was a scratch on her side, so small he could barely see it. "You're right. That'll do you no harm." He set her down, then pulled on his shirt. It was so short now that it barely met his pants. He was beginning to get cold already.

Coalbrow started to get up again. He helped her. She tried to put weight on her wounded leg, and staggered. Limper picked her up and carried her to the horse, Nargri following after. He lifted Coalbrow onto the horse and, when she was in the saddle, said, "Do you think you can stay up there without help?"

Coalbrow nodded, then grabbed onto the saddlehorn. Her face was still too pale, and it shone with sweat. "I hope you're right," Limper said. He looked down at Nargri. "Do you want to ride?"

"No. I've had enough of that horse."

Limper shrugged, then took hold of the reins and led the horse along the trail. From time to time he looked back at Coalbrow. She looked sick, but she kept ahold of the saddlehorn and stayed more or less upright. By this time the sun was setting. The trail was in shadow. Overhead the clear, blue sky grew darker and darker. They reached the road they'd been on before at twilight's end. Then they stopped and rested till the moon came up. Coalbrow and Nargri slept, both wrapped in the one cloak they still had. Limper stayed awake and kept watch. He was cold and hungry, and he kept hearing noises through the river's roar, starting up and looking around. He saw nothing, though. At last the moon rose, dimming the stars, and he woke Coalbrow and Nargri. He helped Coalbrow onto the horse. Nargri asked, "Do we have to keep on?"

"Yes."

"Then I want to ride."

"Can you handle her?" he said to Coalbrow.

Coalbrow nodded. He picked Nargri up and set her in front of Coalbrow. Then he started leading the horse along the road, north, toward Yara Shoi. They went through hills which were lower than before and further back from the road. Trees grew on either side of the road, and the river was soon out of sight behind them, though Limper could still hear the sound of rushing water. His bad leg was bothering him a little, and he went slowly. The road in front of him was pale in the moonlight. The trees on either side were dark. They moved and rustled in a slight, cold wind. Limper started shivering. The hills they passed grew smaller and smaller. By the time the moon set, they were on level ground that was thickly forested. They stopped beside the river, and Coalbrow and Nargri went to sleep again. Limper stayed awake, though he was beginning to have trouble keeping his eyes open. At last at dawn he dozed. When he woke, the sun was well up. The sky above him was bright with light and full of big, ragged clouds. Coalbrow and Nargri were still asleep, underneath the cloak. He stood up, stiff and cold, swore and blew on his hands to warm them. After that he waded into a likely-looking part of the river and caught five fish before his feet got numb. He cleaned the fish with Coalbrow's knife, then made a fire and cooked them. Nargri woke, sniffed and said, "I'm hungry."

"Wake Coalbrow."

She hit Coalbrow with one of her forefeet, and the girl groaned and stirred, then sat up. Her face was flushed, and she was better-looking than usual with that extra color. "How are you?" Limper asked.

"My leg hurts, and I'm thirsty."

Limper took one of the fish off the fire and tossed it toward Nargri, then went over to Coalbrow and helped her get to the river bank. She drank a little water, then moved closer to the fire. Limper gave her a fish and got one for himself. He sat down, his back against a tree and began to eat. Nargri was halfway through the fish he'd given her.

When he was done eating, he licked his fingers. "I wasn't expecting to see you again, Coalbrow. The hairy men said they'd left six of their fellows at the river to take care of you."

Coalbrow shrugged. "I met up with them, after I got back across the river, but I used my bow. I should've used it before. After I put arrows into a couple of them, they stopped trying to bother me. Then I met up with Nargri, and we went looking for you."

"We found out where you'd come out of the river," Nargri said, "and we followed your footprints. Coalbrow's father taught her how to track." She got herself another fish and took a bite out of it.

Coalbrow's face turned bright red. Limper looked over at her and said, "I knew before this that you weren't a boy. I don't intend to give you any trouble about it. It's none of my business. Though I'd be interested in knowing how you got into the habit of wearing men's clothes. You seem pretty used to them."

She shrugged again. "My mother died when I was still young. My father didn't like my mother's relatives, and all his relatives were in the north. So he decided to raise me himself. But he knew nothing about raising girls, so he raised me as a boy. He said it was much easier all around."

"He sounds like a strange man," Limper said.

"He was."

They finished eating. Limper got up and kicked apart the fire, then went and got the horse, which was grazing a short way off. He tightened the saddle cinches, then lifted Coalbrow into the saddle, and they went on, Limper and Nargri walking. The day was sunny and the sky bright blue with grey and white clouds in it. A cold breeze stirred the wood they went through and whirled brown leaves across the road. Limper's eyes were bothering him, and he had a headache. When his leg began to ache, he put Nargri up on the horse, then mounted behind Coalbrow, and they went on, traveling slowly so not to tire the horse. Midway through the morning Nargri said, "Look at that."

Limper looked around. There was a huge, old oak close by the road. A deer skull hung from one of its branches. Both horns were gone. There were streaks of red paint circling the holes where the deer's eyes had been.

"I hope that's a boundary marker," Limper said.

Coalbrow said, "I don't understand why the trolls haven't followed us."

"Maybe they thought we'd caused them enough trouble. Also one of them stuck a spear into their sorcerer by mistake. A religious person might think that was unlucky and a bad way to begin an expedition. It seemed to me that the hairy men took their religion pretty seriously."

They kept on. The country they went through continued to be flat and thickly wooded. Most of the trees had changed color. Once or twice they saw flocks of migrating birds in the sky. Midway through the afternoon they came to a wide, shallow stream, forded it, and made camp on the other side. Limper waded into the stream to catch fish. He had more trouble than usual. Fatigue made his vision blurry and his movements clumsy. Finally he caught three fish, cleaned them and cooked them. After they'd eaten, he lay down in the shade. "One of you keep watch." Then he shut his eyes and went to sleep.

He didn't wake till the next day at dawn. Coalbrow and Nargri were asleep beside him, the one cloak covering all three of them. He lay still for a while, aware of Nargri's small, cool, scaly body curled up next to him, between him and Coalbrow, where she'd get the most warmth. Only her snout stuck out from under the cloak. Coalbrow was sleeping restlessly, murmuring words he couldn't understand. He got up on one elbow. It was still too dark for him to see well. Coalbrow's face was a pale, blurry oval that moved back and forth. He reached over and felt her forehead. It was hot and dry.

"Hell," he said. He got up. The sky was still cloudy, and the air was damp and cold. The fire was out. He went over, rebuilt it, and relit it.

"Limper?"

He looked around. It was Nargri, looking out from under the cloak, her eyes shining in the firelight. "Is Coalbrow sick?"

"I think so." Limper turned back to the fire and put another branch on. "I don't know if the wound's gotten infected or if it's something else. Whatever it is, I don't know how to treat it. How would you like to go down the road and see if you can find any signs of people? I'd better stay with Coalbrow, in case the hairy men show up."

"All right."

"And be careful. I don't want to have to worry about you, too."

"All right."

He turned again and watched Nargri leave.

Shortly after that, Coalbrow woke and sat up. "How are you?" he asked.

"I feel terrible." She felt along her leg and grimaced.

"How is it?"

"I don't think it's any worse than yesterday." She tried to stand and had trouble. Limper came over and gave her a hand, then helped her walk to the river's edge. After she had drunk some water and splashed some more on her face and the back of her neck, Limper carried her back under the trees. He set her down, then said, "It's a good thing there's no one around to watch us. They'd laugh themselves sick at the sight of two cripples helping each other get around."

Coalbrow looked up at him and frowned. "I've noticed that your limp isn't always the same, Holrin. Sometimes it seems you can barely get around, and sometimes you move pretty easily."

"Get that cloak around you. You'll get a cold along with everything else." She wrapped the cloak around her, and Limper said, "The limp's worse when I'm tired and when the weather's bad. When I can't afford to be lame, it gets better. Do you want anything to eat?"

"No."

Limper sat down. "Neither do I. I'm tired of fish."

Coalbrow lay down. After a while she went to sleep.

It was cloudy all day, and from time to time a drizzly rain fell. But it wasn't too cold, and he was pretty comfortable in the shelter of the trees. Around noon he caught a couple of fish and cooked them. Coalbrow woke then and asked him to get her some kind of walking stick. He found a branch that was more or less straight, and she used it to walk off into the woods to relieve herself. When she came back, she drank some water and ate a little fish. Then she lay drowsing, wrapped in the cloak, watching the sky. A little before sunset the rain stopped, and the clouds began to break apart. There were holes that went all the way through to the blue sky, also great rifts Limper could look up into and see layer and layer of cloud, each layer a lighter grey than the one below it. In places the clouds were sunlit, whiter than snow, with their edges outlined in light. All the clouds were moving quickly across the sky and continually changing shape. Finally Coalbrow said, "Most of the time, I don't believe there are any gods."

"Is that so?"

She nodded. "But when the sky looks like that, I think someone must live up there. Look at that cloud, the one that looks like a white cliff. It seems to me someone ought to come walking out to the edge of it, wearing glittering armor."

Limper looked where she was pointing. "Well, I've never seen anything up there except birds and a bat or two at twilight."

"Don't you ever wish you'd see a god?"

Limper scratched his nose. "Not much. From everything I've ever heard, gods are hard to get along with. Let them take care of their business, whatever it may be, and I'll take care of my business."

"What is it?"

"What?"

"Your business. You've never told me."

Limper grinned. "I'm not sure. Smithing, I guess. That's what I was raised to do."

Coalbrow frowned, still looking at the sky. In the west there were rows and rows of small, fat clouds, colored yellow by the setting sun. The sky between the clouds was a very pale blue. "You're a smith, Holrin?"

Limper nodded. "I was one, at least. I haven't done much of anything except travel lately. Why?"

"Because everyone knows that the master smith of Eshgorin is a northerner and lame. From what I've heard, he's been traveling lately." She looked at him, still frowning. "But you don't look old enough to be Limper."

"I'm older than I look." A gust of wind shook the branches above them, and water spattered down on him, hitting his head and running down his neck. "I suppose, since I've found out your secret, you should know mine." He scratched his nose again. "I'm Holrin Limper. I used to be the master smith of Eshgorin." He looked over at Coalbrow. She was still frowning.

"You're a smith, and you have no interest in the gods?"

Limper nodded.

"But smithing is a holy craft, like poetry and making prophecies."

"I never knew what that meant. All I know is I've done smithwork most of my life. I do it because I do it. As for what it means—" He shrugged. "The king of Eshgorin thought I worked for his glory. I've had days when I thought I worked for my glory. But who can say for sure? How are you feeling?"

"Well enough." She moved slightly and pulled the cloak closer around her. Her cheeks were red. Her dark hair was wet and curling a little. "I knew a man in Anyar, who had one of your swords. He

said you'd made it, anyway. There were little
animals on the guards, covered with gilt. I liked it.
You feel there's nothing holy about making
something like that?"

Limper grinned, then looked out at the river,
which was in shadow and shone dully, like tarnished silver. "There are days when I'm working
and everything goes right, and I feel some god behind me. I even feel his breath on my back. I
think, if I straighten up and turn around, I'll see
him—taller than any man, with eyes like fire. So I
keep working, and I don't lift my head till I know
he's gone."

"Why?"

Limper looked at her. "Why what?"

"Why don't you turn around?"

Limper shrugged. "I think, if I ever turn to face
the god, he'll tell me what he wants from me in
return for the gift he's given me." He held out
his hands. They were long and bony with big
knuckles. There was a white burn-scar on the back
of one of them, and there was dirt or soot under all
the nails. "In return for the skill in these."

Coalbrow looked at him, frowning. "What do
you think he wants?"

"Me. My services till I die. And I won't serve
him, any more than I'll serve the king of Eshgorin.
I don't intend to spend my life at an anvil."

"Most of the time when people say, 'the gods
want such-and-such', What they mean is, *they* want
such-and-such."

Limper laughed. "You're crazy." He stood up.
"You'd better get some rest. I'll go get supper."

He went into the river and caught two more fish.
When he got back to the campfire, Coalbrow was
asleep, and Nargri was there, watching her.

"I found a farm, Limper, half a day from here. I watched the people for a while. They looked friendly enough to me. How's Coalbrow?"

Limper shrugged. "She seems to be all right."

He cleaned the fish and cooked them. Coalbrow woke and ate a little. After supper he untied the bandages around her leg and looked at the wound. It didn't look infected or unusually inflamed. He washed out the bandages and rebound the wound. "There's nothing wrong there," he told Coalbrow. "Maybe what you have is a cold."

Nargri went to sleep early. Limper stayed up and kept watch. Finally he lay down, but he was restless and soon sat up. There were a few white puffs of cloud here and there above him. Most of the sky was clear and bright with stars. "Well, what do you want from me?" he asked, looking up. "And what did I ever do to you, either good or bad, to deserve the gift you gave me?"

He got no answer to his questions. After a while he lay down and went to sleep.

AT THE FARM

The next morning Nargri woke him, hitting him in the side. He groaned and rolled over. She hit him again. He sat up, grabbed her and said, "Do you want to be tossed in the river?"

"No."

He set her down. "Then don't poke people."

Coalbrow was at the fire, adding more wood to it. "How are you?" he asked.

"Better. I think you're right. What I have is a cold."

Limper stood up. The day was cool and bright. The river glittered in the sunlight, and sunlight shone through the brown leaves above him, making them glow. He felt hungry, but he didn't want to eat any more fish.

Coalbrow said, "I think I'll wait to eat till we reach the farm Nargri found. If I eat more fish, I'll grow scales."

"What's wrong with scales?" Nargri asked.

"They'd look strange on us," Limper said and went to saddle the horse.

Coalbrow had trouble mounting. She winced as she settled in the saddle and bit her lip. Limper looked up at her. "You're sure you'll be able to ride?"

"Yes. Let's go."

He picked up Nargri and handed her to Coalbrow, then took the horse's reins and led it toward the road.

"Aren't you going to ride?" Nargri asked.

"I feel like walking for a while. My leg feels fine today."

They went slowly, Limper leading the horse. The road went northwest through brown and yellow woods. A wind blew fitfully. Overhead fat, round, white clouds traveled across the sky. From time to time he looked back at Coalbrow. Her face was still too red. After an hour or so he noticed that her shoulders were sagging. "How are you?"

"Fine. Fine."

They kept traveling. After another hour Coalbrow looked pretty sick, her face pale and her eyes unfocused. "We'd better stop," Limper said.

"No. It's only a dizzy feeling. I don't want to stop."

Limper shrugged and kept going. Shortly after that Nargri cried, "Limper."

Limper looked back and saw Coalbrow sagging to one side. He moved as fast as he could and caught her before she fell. He lifted her the rest of the way out of the saddle and carried her to the side of the road, laid her in the grass, then felt her forehead. It was hot and dry. She was breathing normally. He felt her pulse, holding her wrist the way a doctor had showed him back in Eshgorin. It seemed a little fast to him, but he wasn't sure. He rocked back on his heels and listened. He could hear birds calling and the rustle of leaves, but not the sound of water. "How far is that farm, Nargri?"

"Half an hour, maybe more."

He went back to the horse and lifted Nargri down. "You watch Coalbrow." He gathered the reins, mounted, kicked the horse, and kept kicking till the horse was galloping. A little further on the road turned. He glanced back and saw Nargri, a little, dark shape in the middle of the road. She was up on her hind legs, her head held high and turned toward him. Then branches hid her. He looked ahead. At the next turn of the road he saw smoke, a grey line trailing across the blue sky. The road went toward the smoke. He slowed the horse to a canter. Soon after that he saw stumps along the road, where trees had been lumbered. Then he came to fields of stubble with cattle grazing in them. The road went through a grove of oaks. A pair of hogs hunted acorns under the trees. He startled them, and they squealed and fled. On the other side of the grove was a green home field and, beyond that, farm buildings. He slowed the horse to a trot and tugged at his sword to make sure it wouldn't stick, if he had to take it out. When he reached the farm, he stopped and yelled, "Hello?"

Two men stepped out from behind one of the buildings. One of them had a pitchfork, and the other had a boar hunting spear. They were both young, 18 or 19, both tall, and yellow-haired. Their faces were sunburnt red.

"What do you want?" the man with the pitchfork asked. He spoke the language of the northerners.

"A friend of mine is sick a little way down the road. I need help. Do you have a cart?"

The men looked at one another. "It might be a trap," the man with the pitchfork said.

The second man nodded.

"Do you have a cart?" Limper asked again.

"Yes," the first man said. "But we haven't agreed to help you."

"Get your damn cart ready. I'll get in it with you. If there's a trap, you can kill me."

The men looked at each other again. Behind Limper a woman said, "That seems fair enough."

Limper looked back. The woman stood at the door of one of the buildings, wiping her hands on her skirt. She was tall and yellow-haired and looked several years older than the men. "There've been robbers around. We've all learned to be careful. Hitch Coppermane and Whitefoot to the cart, Andringir."

The man with the pitchfork nodded and turned away.

"How far is your friend?" the woman asked.

"Half an hour to the south."

"What's wrong with him?"

He dismounted and faced the woman. "He got wounded in Troll Wood, and he's running a fever."

"How many of you are there?"

"Two. My friend and me."

The other man came over to stand by the woman. They looked like brother and sister, both of them tall and fair and sunburnt. The woman's hair was paler, and her eyes were darker, and she was much the better-looking of the two.

"I'm Holrin Gergitsson," Limper said.

The woman smiled. "I'm named Sotla, but my

father nicknamed me Sunlily. This is my brothe.
Gerthal. The other fellow is my brother Andringir."

"You are lucky to get out of Troll Wood alive,"
Gerthal said. "The trolls are brave, when they
meet small parties."

Limper grinned. "I found that out." He kept
looking at Sotla. She was wearing one narrow silver bracelet, and her belt had a gilt buckle. Her
hair shone more brightly than the metal, or so it
seemed to Limper.

The other man, Andringir, came back, leading
two horses that were hitched to a small cart. There
was a sword at his side that hadn't been there before. Limper tied his horse to the cart and climbed
in. Gerthal climbed in after him, still holding the
boar spear.

"I'll see you in a while," Sotla said, and
Andringir led the horses down the road.

The going was rough. The cart jolted over
bumps and ruts. Gerthal kept a tight grip on the
spear and watched Limper closely. As for Limper,
he watched the horses and the grass-grown road in
front of them. The horses must have been descend-
ed from northern ponies, for they were on the
small side and shaggy-coated with dark stripes
down their backs. One of them was brown. The
other one was yellow with a thick, bristly, red-
brown mane. Limper tugged at a hangnail, trying
to pull it off. After a while he noticed there was
blood on his hands. The hangnail was torn and
bleeding. He wiped the blood off and looked back
at the road.

"Why are you so uneasy?" Gerthal asked. "Are
you expecting trouble of some kind?"

Limper looked at him. "For all I know, my friend's dying or dead."

Gerthal nodded. "I guess that makes sense."

Soon after that Limper saw Nargri in the road ahead of them.

Andringir stopped and grabbed at his sword's hilt.

"What is that?" Gerthal asked.

"My dragon," Limper said. "Don't worry about her. She's harmless."

"Your dragon?" Gerthal frowned. "Our father did a lot of traveling before he settled down. He said there were no dragons nor dwarves nor elves. Those were all old wives' tales, he said, that no man believed who'd been around and learned enough to form wise opinions."

"Well, if she's not a dragon, what is she?"

"I don't know," Gerthal said. "But that thing's too small to be a dragon."

"You two can argue this," Andringir said. He let go of his sword and led the horses on.

When the cart got closer, Nargri ran to the side of the road. Limper saw Coalbrow sitting there, her back against a tree trunk, her bow in her hands. "It's all right," he shouted. Coalbrow smiled. Her face was flushed red.

Andringir stopped the horses. Limper swung himself over the cart's side onto the road. Andringir whirled and pulled out his sword. Limper stood still. Something sharp and hard pricked him between the shoulder blades. "Slowly," Gerthal said.

"The way you act, robbers are as common around here as rats in a grainery. Can I get my friend?"

Andringir nodded. Limper went to Coalbrow.

He helped her up and helped her walk to the cart. By the time she lay down on the cart's floor, her face was pale again. Limper lifted Nargri into the cart, then climbed in and sat down beside Coalbrow. "How are you?"

"All right," Coalbrow said, then shut her eyes. Limper felt her forehead. It was still dry, and it seemed to him it was hotter than before.

Andringir turned the horses and started back home.

"You're sure that's a dragon?" Gerthal said.

Limper nodded. "Well, it's certainly something different. I'm willing to call it a dragon. It's a good thing my father is dead, though. He hated being wrong."

Nargri moved closer to Limper. He touched her lightly, then leaned back against the side of the cart. He couldn't stretch his legs out, because Coalbrow was in the way. Nobody said anything more. When they got to the farm, Limper carried Coalbrow into the main building. Sotla was there, putting a new blanket in a sleeping cabinet. She looked around, then finished spreading the blanket and stood back so Limper could lift Coalbrow into the cabinet. She looked at Coalbrow, who was a pale greenish color, and clicked her tongue. "You see to your horse, Holrin. I'll see to your friend."

Limper hesitated. Nargri came inside, Gerthal behind her. "What's that?" Sotla asked.

"A dragon," Gerthal said. "Or so this fellow says."

"Well, whatever it is, I don't want it in my house."

"All right," Limper said. "Come on, Nargri." He went out, and Nargri followed.

Andringir was leading the horses back to the

barn. They went with him. Limper helped him un-·
hitch the cart horses and let them loose in the
home field. Then he unsaddled his own horse.
When he was done, he said, "Is there anything
else I can do?"

"Well, I was going to spend this morning cleaning the sty. How do you feel about pig dung?"

Limper grinned. "Give me a shovel."

He spent the rest of the morning shoveling
dung, while Nargri watched from atop the pigs'
house. A little after noon they went in to eat. Coalbrow was sleeping in the cabinet, and Sotla and
Gerthal were at the table. "I still don't want that
beast of yours in my house," Sotla said.

Limper looked down at Nargri, who looked up at
him. "She has to eat."

"I'll put a bowl outside."

"All right." Limper nodded toward the door.
Nargri hissed loudly, then went out. He went out
after her.

"I can see what kind of friend you are," Nargri
said in the language of the dragons.

"We can't afford to quarrel with these people till
Coalbrow is able to travel."

"I don't like being treated like an animal. We
dragons were building cities when you men were
living in huts made out of leaves. I'm a person, and
I smell a lot better than you do right now."

"Be patient."

"You can say that. You're going to be inside."

"I'm sorry," Limper said and went into the
house. There was food on the table: hot pork, cab-
bage, onions and bread, also a big jug of beer. Sotla
served him, then asked, "What does your beast
eat?"

"The same food as we do."

She put bread and onions in a bowl along with a little pork and took it outside. When she came back in, she said, "You didn't tell us your friend was a girl."

"You found that out, did you?" Limper drank a little beer. Both Gerthal and Andringir looked surprised.

"The wound she has looks all right to me," Sotla went on. "I don't think it's infected. But it's big enough so she'll need time to recover from it."

Limper nodded and ate some of the pork. He felt suddenly tired. His eyes hurt, and he didn't want to go out into the glare of day. "I don't think I'll be able to help you this afternoon," he said to Andringir.

Andringir nodded.

After he was done eating Limper lay down on a bench against the back wall and went to sleep. He didn't wake till late in the evening. A fire was burning in the firepit. The two brothers were sitting at the table playing chess, and Sotla was sitting close to the fire, twisting wool into yarn. Limper watched her for a while. Her long, plaited hair shone like gold, and the bracelet on her wrist glittered when she moved her hand. At last she looked up and smiled. Her mouth, Limper noticed, was full-lipped and redder than was usual among northern women, who didn't paint their mouths. "Do you want anything to eat?"

Limper sat up. "Yes. How's my friend?"

Sotla put down her spindle. "Asleep. She was awake for a while and ate."

"Good. I'll be back." Limper got up and went outside. A brisk, cold wind was blowing. The moon was up, half full, lighting huge, ragged clouds. "Nargri?"

Nargri ran toward him out of the darkness. "Limper. I'm freezing."

He picked her up and held her. Her skin felt colder than usual. He went back inside, still carrying her. Andringir and Gerthal had stopped their game, and Sotla was setting food on the table. She looked up and frowned.

"If you want, I'll sleep in the barn, Sotla. Nargri can't stay outside alone."

"I'm not having a beast like that in my house," Sotla said. "If you want to bed down in hay, that's fine with me." She filled a plate with food and a cup with beer. "Here."

Limper put Nargri down and took the plate and cup. "Thank you. Good night."

Nargri ran ahead of him out of the house and across the yard to the barn. He opened the door, lifting the latch with an elbow since both his hands were full, and she ran in. He followed. The door swung in, blown by the wind, and shut with a bang. Limper jumped and spilled a little beer. He heard a click as the latch fell into place. He was in darkness. He stood still a moment. The air was warm and stank of hay and dung. He took a swallow of beer, then called, "Nargri?"

"Here, Limper. I've found the ladder into the loft."

He followed the sound of her voice to the ladder and set the cup down there. After that he carried the plate of food up into the loft, then went back down for the cup.

The loft was almost full, but there was room for them at its edge. Limper ate and drank, sitting next to the ladder's top, his legs swinging in dark space. Below him he heard a horse moving in a stall. After a while his eyes adjusted to the darkness, and he saw moonlight coming through cracks around the door and between the shutters on the loft window.

"I don't like that woman," Nargri said, her mouth full of mutton.

"I can't understand why not." Limper finished eating and stretched out in the hay. The rafters above him were just barely visible, lit by the dim moonlight. Beneath him the hay was dry and prickly. The air was full of dust and the smell of hay. Nargri settled herself beside him.

"Do you like her, Limper?"

"I find it hard to think badly of anyone who's that beautiful."

"My mother told me that males count appearance more than they should."

"We're not the only ones. Remember Shendil, who fell in love with her own construction because he was beautiful?"

Nargri sniffed, sneezed, then snuggled closer to him. Limper put his arm around her. Her scaly skin felt smooth and cool. After a while he went to sleep.

He woke early in the morning, when sunlight began to shine into the barn through cracks in the walls. Nargri was still asleep, curled up, her tail over her nose. He heard someone moving below him and looked over the loft's edge. Gerthal was milking the cow in the end stall. Limper picked up the plate and cup from supper and went down the ladder. Gerthal nodded to him and kept milking. The horses were all gone from their stalls. When he got outside he saw them grazing in the home field. There was a cold wind blowing; it ruffled the horses' manes and tails and made Limper's hair flap around his neck. He went to the farmhouse, walking slowly, looking around at the farm buildings with their dark plank walls and brown turf roofs. Pigs grunted in the sty, and a big grey goose pecked at something by the farmhouse door. Inside the house there was food on the table. Coalbrow was awake and sitting up in bed. In one corner of the room a woman sat at a loom, weaving. She looked around briefly. She wasn't a northerner. Her ruddy face was too wide, and her blue-grey eyes were almond-shaped and slanted. Her long, plaited hair was light brown. Most likely she was a slave.

"How are you?" Limper asked Coalbrow.

"Better."

He picked up a piece of cheese from the table and went over to sit by her. "Where's Sotla?"

"Feeding the geese, I think. Where's Nargri?"

"Asleep in the barn."

"Sotla was asking me why you had a pet like that. She doesn't like snakes or lizards."

"Well, she has a right to her opinion. I have days when I like dragons better than people. In some ways, they're easier to understand."

Coalbrow frowned.

Limper finished the cheese, then said, "Dragons usually say what's on their minds, for one thing. You don't have to worry about what they're thinking, because they'll tell you."

"They're lucky if they know what they're thinking. Do you?"

Limper shrugged, then looked around at the table. There were apples on it as well as cheese, also bread and dried fish. "Sometimes I know. I'm going to go eat."

Coalbrow nodded, and Limper left her.

Sotla came in while he was eating. She was

wearing a bright blue dress with elaborate gold brooches pinned above her breasts. Her belt buckle was shaped like a dragon coiled around itself. It was made of bronze, covered with gilt, and the dragon's eyes were amber. She stopped, sniffed and grimaced. "You'd better take a bath, Holrin, as soon as you've eaten." She looked him over. "You ought to be able to wear Andringir's clothes." She looked to the woman at the loom. "Go and tell Mirhav to get the bathhouse ready."

The woman nodded, got up and went out. Sotla refilled Limper's cup with beer. "Your friend Coalbrow's fever is gone, though it may be back this evening. That's the way with fevers. I'll get you some clean clothes and a razor. Your hair needs trimming."

She left him. He finished eating, then looked over at Coalbrow. She was watching him and frowning. "What is it?" he asked.

"Don't you mind the way she orders you around?"

He shrugged. "Why should I? She hasn't told me to do anything I don't want to do."

Coalbrow kept frowning.

"What would be the point of refusing to take a bath? I don't like smelling like pig dung."

"My father said, slaves do without respect because they have to, but a free man has a choice."

"Well, your father was a soldier. He could defend his honor. I find it easier to forget about such things."

Sotla came back with clothes, a comb, a razor and a mirror made of polished steel. "The bathhouse is out back."

Limper took the bundle from her and went outside. The bathhouse was beside a stream which ran in back of the farm buildings. Grey geese splashed in the shallows and pecked at food on the bank. On the stream's far side was the forest, all of its leaves yellow or brown. As Limper went toward the bathhouse, a man came out of it. He looked like the woman who'd been weaving: wide-faced and brown-haired. His clothes were faded and patched. A scar ran down the side of his face across one corner of his mouth, making his lower lip twist down. It looked to Limper as if a sword had made the scar. "Were you ever a soldier?" he asked the man when they met.

The man stopped. After a moment he nodded.

"I thought so."

"Not for long, though," the man said. He spoke the language of the northerners with a thick accent. "The first battle I was in my side lost, and I was taken captive."

Limper looked away from him, up at the sky, which was bright and cloudless from horizon to horizon. "That has happened to lots of men," he said finally.

"That may be," the man said. "I've never heard that a thing is made better by being common."

"You're probably right," Limper said and went on to the bathhouse. The stones on the hearth were hot. There was a barrel full of water. All he had to do was undress and pour water over the stones till the house was full of steam. He scrubbed off the outer layers of dirt and sweated the dirt out of his pores, then he went through the bathhouse's back door. He waded into the stream till he was waist deep and splashed the clear, fast-running water all over himself. An acorn plopped into the stream next to him. He looked up. There was a squirrel in the tree above him. It chittered and flicked its bushy tail before disappearing. Limper grinned.

When he began to feel the water's coldness, he got back into the bathhouse, found a towel and dried himself. By that time the steam was gone, and the bathhouse walls were covered with water. He combed his hair, then wiped the mirror off and cut his hair's ragged ends. After that he trimmed his beard. It didn't look much better short, so he shaved it off, leaving only a moustache. Then he got the clean clothes, which he'd left outside on a hook by the door. He put them on. They were a little large, but not so much as to be really noticeable. The shirt was green with gold embroidery around the neck, and the belt buckle was a bronze stag, the work of the herding people. He pulled on his boots and went back to the farmhouse. Sotla was starting to clear the table. She looked him over. "I must say, you're a lot better looking than I expected."

He grinned.

"But why did you shave off your beard?"

Limper shrugged. "Why not?"

"Moustaches are all right for young men, but a full grown man looks better with a beard."

"That may be." There was still food on the table. Limper took some bread and cheese and a dried fish. "I'd better go find your brothers and offer to help them with their work. Guests who bring nothing and do nothing are never welcome."

"Very well," Sotla said.

He went back to the barn. Nargri was sitting just inside the open door, safe from the wind, basking in the sunlight. He gave her the food, and she started eating. "I'll see you later," he said, then went looking for Sotla's brothers. He found them finally in the near field, gathering the last of the hay. Mirhav was with them. They gave Limper a pitchfork, and he spent the morning heaving hay up into the cart. At noon the slave-woman brought them food. They ate quickly and then went back to work. Limper was having trouble using his pitchfork. Andringir had to stop work several times and show him how to lift the hay without losing it. By midafternoon his back and arms hurt, and he had to rest after lifting each forkful into the cart. A little before sunset, they were done. Mirhav drove the cart back, and the rest of them trudged home behind him.

"I just realized that's my shirt," Andringir said to Limper. "And you've probably ruined it, sweating in it."

"Sotla must like you," Gerthal said, "if she's dressing you so finely."

Andringir frowned. "We'd better tell you, Holrin. Our mother is off visiting some neighbors right now. She's hoping she can arrange a marriage for Sotla while she's there."

"Besides, you already have a woman," Gerthal said.

"I do? Who?"

Gerthal looked surprised. "Coalbrow."

"She might have a few words to say about that."

They got home and ate dinner. Limper said goodnight to Coalbrow, then went out to the barn, taking food for Nargri. It was a little after sunset, and the western sky was still pink. The evening star was shining. Nargri was in the barn, up in the loft. Limper took the food up to her. She ate it quickly. When she was done she said, "How long are we going to be here?"

"A few more days."

"I don't like this place."

Limper nodded. "I'm going out for a while."

Nargri looked at him for a moment. "All right."

He left the barn and went behind the main house, along the stream. The trees rustled in the wind, and he felt cold. His back ached, as did his bad leg, and he was very tired. He stopped and turned, looking at the farm's buildings, dark against the western sky. Smoke rose from two chimneys. Red firelight shone out of several windows. After a while he saw someone coming toward him. There was still enough light so he could make out Sotla's pale hair and the dim gleam of her jewelry. "Stasa told me she saw someone outside," she said.

"I was looking at your farm and thinking that I haven't much to show for my life."

"What do you expect? There's a limit to how much a traveler can carry. People have to settle down in order to prosper. Or so I think. What you ought to do, Holrin, is find yourself an heiress. You're not bad looking, and there's something likeable about you."

"People are always giving me good advice."

After a moment Sotla said, "You know the saying, don't you? To advise a wise man, you have to be wise yourself. But anyone can advise a fool."

Limper grinned. "I'm going in. It's cold out here."

Sotla walked with him as far as the farmhouse, then said good night. He went on to the barn and climbed up into the loft. He went to sleep almost at once, but he slept restlessly and had bad dreams. He woke in the middle of the night, covered with sweat, with Nargri shaking his arm. "Limper, what's wrong?"

After a moment Limper said, "I dreamt I was in the smithy at Eshgorin working, and the god was behind me."

"Which god?"

"I don't know. Go back to sleep, Nargri."

She curled up next to him. He lay awake a while, staring up at the dark roof. Finally he went to sleep.

The next day was overcast and cold. He went with Andringir into the forest and cut wood, loading it into the cart. He was stiff from working the day before, and he wasn't used to swinging an ax, so he had a hard time of it at first. After half an hour or so, Andringir said, "What do you do for a living, Holrin? You can't handle a pitchfork or an ax, and I don't see how a lame man can be a soldier. If you're a peddler, you're the first one I've ever seen without a pack."

Limper stopped to rest and rub his hands on his pants. There were blisters forming on his left palm, where he had fewer calluses. "I'm a smith."

"With no tools?"

"I lost them." He started swinging the ax again. The axblade stuck in the wood, and he had trouble yanking it free. After a moment he looked at Andringir, who was frowning. "What's that look for?"

"My father did some smithing. We still have his tools, and we have things that need mending."

Limper nodded. "I'll mend them if I can."

By late afternoon the cart was almost full of wood, and they went back to the farm. Andringir drove, while Limper went to sleep, sitting in the back of the cart, surrounded by the wood. He woke when the cart stopped moving, groaned and climbed out. The sky was still grey, except in the

west, where the clouds had split apart so he could
see the sun. He ached all over, and his hands and
arms were getting stiff again. He helped Andringir
unhitch the horses, fumbling at the harness
buckles, and then hung the harness up, while
Andringir took the horses to the stream. After that
he went into the farmhouse. Gerthal and Sotla
were sitting at the table, eating. Coalbrow was sitting with them. She looked as if she'd taken a bath.
Her dark, short hair was clean and neatly combed,
and she was wearing a brown dress. Sotla had on a
green dress and a necklace made of silver coins.
Limper stopped and stared at Coalbrow. "You
certainly look different in that."

"I don't like it, but Sotla said my own clothes
needed washing."

"She's probably right." He sat down and helped
himself to mutton and onions.

Andringir came in a moment later. "I found out
that Holrin is a smith," he said as he sat down.

"That's a good skill to have," Sotla said. "A man
can earn his keep and more, smithing."

"He's agreed to do some work for us." Andringir
poured himself some ale and tasted it. He glanced
over to Coalbrow and seemed to notice her for the
first time. He opened his mouth to say something,
then shut it and went back to eating. After that he
kept glancing at her. After a while Coalbrow's face
got red.

"Why are you looking at me that way,
Andringir?"

Andringir flushed and said nothing. Sotla
laughed. "He's probably noticed that you're better
looking than you were before."

Andringir glared at Sotla.

Limper glanced at Coalbrow. She did look like a

woman for the first time, pretty enough except for her strange, thick, black eyebrows. She was a little too thin for his liking, though.

"Do you want to play chess?" Andringir asked his brother. Gerthal nodded. They got out the chessboard and set out the pieces.

Coalbrow said, "I'm going back to bed." She stood up, then swayed a little and put her hand on the table.

Andringir stood, almost knocking over the bench. "Let me help you."

"No. Holrin will."

Andringir flushed and glared at Limper. Limper set down his cup, got up and helped Coalbrow to the sleeping cabinet. As soon as she was settled, Coalbrow whispered, "Let's get out of here."

Limper shook his head. "You're still sick, and I've promised to do some smithwork for these people."

"All right. But hurry with the smithwork. I'll get well as quickly as I can."

Limper grinned, then left her. He got some food and a cup of ale from the table and went out to the barn. Nargri was sitting just inside the door. "It's about time. I'm getting bored here."

He gave her the food and drank half the ale while she ate. Then she drank the rest of the ale. "Limper?" she asked after they were settled in the loft.

"Yes?"

"Are you thinking of staying here?"

He looked up at the rafters. "Well, we could find worse places."

"Where? I'm not going to spend the rest of my life living in a barn like a rat."

"Aren't you tired of traveling, Nargri?"

"Not tired enough to stay here."

Limper clasped his hands behind his head. He could smell his own stale sweat as well as the hay. He heard a rustling sound on the barn floor: one of the barn rats, running over the straw. The cow moved, and her halter clinked softly. "We're far enough north, so I don't have to worry about the king of Eshgorin. And we're going to have to spend the winter somewhere. Why not here?"

"No," Nargri said.

"We don't have to make a decision tonight. Get some sleep."

"I'll still say 'no' tomorrow." Nargri curled up next to him. Soon after that Limper went to sleep. He woke in the middle of the night. Rain beat on the roof above him, and the wet wind blew in the loft window. He listened to the rain a while, then went back to sleep.

In the morning it was still raining, a misty drizzle that hid the distances and made everything nearby look dim and grey. After breakfast Andringir showed him the smithy. It was behind the barn: a little, low hut with cobwebs in the corners and a musty, moldy stink. Dust covered the smith-tools, the iron ingots, and the charcoal heap. Limper looked around, hefted the hammers, and tried the bellows to make sure they still worked. Then he wiped his hands on his pants and nodded. "I can work here."

"Is Coalbrow your lover?" Andringir asked.

"Ask her. Now, what do you want mended?"

Andringir flushed. "I'll have Gerthal bring you everything."

Limper nodded, then set to work building a fire in the forge. Nargri came in as soon as Andringir left. "Can I watch?"

Limper nodded and kept working on the fire. When it was burning well, he wiped the dust off the tools. Gerthal came in, carrying a big kettle and a pitchfork with two broken tines. "There's more."

"Get it." Limper took the kettle and turned it over. It was made of sheets of iron welded together, and one of the seams had opened, making a long, narrow hole. "That's easy to fix." He set the kettle down and looked at the pitchfork. Gerthal came back in, carrying a plowshare that was badly twisted. "What happened to that? It looks as if you tried to plow through a boulder."

"That's what happened, more or less. What're you going to do about Andringir and Coalbrow? I've never seen him in a state like this before."

"First of all, that's Coalbrow's problem more than mine. And second, I like quiet when I work. Get out."

Gerthal flushed, then left.

"Whenever you get in a smithy, you start giving orders," Nargri said. "But you don't do it outside."

"When I'm in a smithy, I know what to do and how to do it. Outside I'm never sure. Now, shut up."

He repaired the pitchfork first, making new tines from the iron he found in the smithy. The iron was much too soft. He had to heat it and beat it flat. He laid the flat piece of iron on the fire to case-harden it. Then he cooled it and cut it into strips. He twisted several of the strips together, so they made a complex spiral. He made two of these spirals, heated them and beat them flat, then welded them onto the pitchfork. When he was done, he straightened up, stretched and noticed Coalbrow standing in the doorway, still wearing the brown dress. "Well?" he said.

"When are we going?"

"I think Limper wants to stay," Nargri said.

Coalbrow grimaced. "Is that true?"

"I've thought of it." He put the pitchfork to one side and put the plowshare on the coals to heat up. "Why not?"

"For one thing, I don't like this place," Coalbrow said. "Nor does Nargri. For another thing, do you really think you can stay in a country smithy and mend pots and plowshares?"

Limper shrugged, looking at the plowshare. "Why not?"

"I've heard travelers talk about the things you made at Eshgorin. There was a tree full of golden birds that sang and an iron dragon with a furnace inside it, so it spewed smoke and fire."

"I told the king that real dragons didn't spit fire. But he never listened to what I said."

"You can't do work like that here."

"I'm not sure I want to."

"Why? Do you think this world is so full of wonders that it needs no more?"

Limper wiped his hands, then looked at the forge fire and frowned. Finally he shrugged. "What use are things like that, anyway? I know Sotla needs her pot, and her brothers need the pitchfork and the plowshare. But who needs a golden bird that sings?"

"You worry about the strangest things," Coalbrow said.

Nargri was sitting on one of the tool shelves. She stirred and stretched, then resettled herself. "It's my aunt's fault, Coalbrow. She took Limper in when he was young and impressionable. My mother says my aunt doubts everything. She should've been a philosopher, my mother says, but she doubted the usefulness of philosophy, so she became a metalsmith."

"Anyway," Limper said, "only a king could afford something like the iron dragon, and I'm not going to work for another king. They're too set in their ways."

"Then set up shop in a market town and make swords," Coalbrow said. "You should've heard that man in Anyar brag about the sword he had, that Holrin Limper had made. The blade was as hard as adamant, he said, but not brittle. It was as sharp as a good razor, and it held its edge for I forget how long. Come to Yara Shoi with me. There are plenty of soldiers there, who'd be glad to buy good swords."

Limper scratched his head. "I'm not sure that I want to make weapons. I don't much like fighting."

"That's my aunt," Nargri said. "If she believes in anything at all, it's peacefulness. My mother says that's what happens when you doubt everything. There's nothing you think is worth fighting for."

Coalbrow shrugged. "Make jewelry then. I saw the animals on the hilt of that fellow's sword in Anyar. They were so finely made I could count the claws on their feet and the teeth in their mouths. If you can do that, you can make jewelry."

Limper frowned. "I don't remember making a swordhilt like that. I think that fellow was mistaken. He had some other smith's sword." He looked at the plowshare. It had begun to glow. He got tongs and pulled it from the forge, laid it on the anvil and started to beat it straight.

Coalbrow stood watching him. After a while she said, "I'm feeling tired. I'll finish this conversation later."

Limper nodded and kept working. When he was

done and looked up, Coalbrow was gone.

The forge fire was beginning to go out. He put new charcoal on it and worked the bellows till all the coals were glowing brightly.

"Do you really think you could stay here and mend pots?" Nargri asked.

Limper shrugged. "I don't know. Probably not." He went to the smithy door and looked out. A fine, misty rain fell. Rain beaded a spider-web under the smithy eave. The grass glistened with water, and the path in front of him was full of puddles. "Don't you envy people who live in one place and work hard and don't ask a lot of questions about life?"

"No," said Nargri.

Limper turned and looked at her. "Why not?"

"I like traveling, though I get homesick from time to time. As for hard work, I can't say I've learned to like it yet. Maybe I will someday. And my mother says that only two kinds of beings ask questions—dragons and men. That's what sets us apart from animals. I don't understand you, Limper. Why don't you like what you are?"

"I'd better get that kettle mended," Limper said.

Sotla came in early in the afternoon, as he was finishing with the kettle. She brought bread and cheese and a jug of ale. She set down the food and watched him till he was done, then said, "You seem pretty skillful to me, Holrin, and this district needs a smith. Why don't you stay?"

"I've been thinking about it." He stretched and kneaded his right arm, which was aching. Then he looked at her. Today she wore a red gown, a pair of gilt bracelets and the belt with the dragon buckle. Even in the dim smithy her pale hair shone. "I can't remember when I saw someone as lovely as you, Sotla."

She smiled. Nargri made a "pft" noise, and Sotla looked at her. "You have that awful lizard here."

"I'd better tell you—Nargri can understand what you're saying," Limper said after a moment. "She knows three languages, and her people are wiser than we are."

"True," Nargri said in the language of the northerners.

Sotla looked startled. "It talks."

Limper nodded.

"Well, my father said there are men in the south, who can train birds to talk. So I suppose someone could teach a lizard to talk. But why would anyone bother?"

Limper shook his head. "No."

"I saw one of those birds in Hwara, when I was looking for you," Nargri said. "There was a man in the street, who had two monkeys that did tumbling tricks and a black bird in a cage that made obscene comments."

Sotla stood, her mouth open, staring at Nargri.

"The dragons are people, not animals," Limper said.

Sotla shook her head. "It doesn't make sense." She turned and walked out.

Limper sighed, then sat down on the floor, his back against the wall, his legs stretched out in front of him. His bad leg felt fine in spite of the weather, but his arms and shoulders felt terrible. "I'm going to have to start working regularly. I'm getting unused to it." The food Sotla brought was on the shelf next to him. He broke off a piece of cheese and ate it. "Sotla's certainly beautiful, but

I'm beginning to think she's a little narrow-minded."

Nargri came over and helped herself to some cheese. "My mother says that people who stay put grow stupid, because they never have anything new to think about. She says that dragons were a lot smarter in the old days, when they lived above ground and traveled a lot."

"That sounds like one of your mother's sayings." Limper drank some ale. "Maybe Coalbrow is right, and I should go to Yara Shoi and look for work." He drank more ale.

"That sounds like a good idea to me," Nargri said, her mouth full of cheese.

After they'd finished eating, Limper ground the pitchfork's tines till they were pointed. Then he cleaned up the smithy and went back to the farmhouse, Nargri beside him. The rain had stopped, but it was still misty out. When they reached the farmhouse door, Nargri stopped. "Come on in," Limper said.

"All right, but if there's any trouble, it's your fault."

Inside Sotla was setting food out for supper. Coalbrow, Andringir and Gerthal were all sitting at the table. "How are you feeling, Coalbrow?" Limper said.

"Pretty well."

"When do you want to leave?"

Coalbrow looked at him, then smiled. "Tomorrow will be soon enough."

"You're sure you can travel?"

"Yes."

"No," Andringir said. "You're still sick, Coalbrow. Anybody can see that."

Coalbrow shook her head.

"I think you're wrong," Sotla said. "You're still weak."

"Let's wait till tomorrow and decide then." Limper sat down, and Nargri climbed up onto the bench beside him.

Sotla frowned. "I said I didn't want that thing in my house."

"Nargri's a person, not a thing," Limper said.

Sotla folded her arms. "Whatever it is, it goes out."

Limper sighed and stood. "Come on, Nargri. We'll eat in the barn."

Coalbrow got up. "I'll go too."

"No," Andringir said. "Sotla, let the lizard stay."

Sotla clicked her tongue. "Oh, all right. Sit down, all of you."

After they ate supper. When supper was over, Coalbrow said, "I'm going to need my own clothes tomorrow, Sotla."

Sotla shook her head. "They're still dirty, though I've washed them once, and the pants are torn. You'd better take one of my dresses."

"No."

"Why not? You look better this way. Ask Andringir."

"No." Coalbrow's face got red. "I can't walk in this thing. I keep tripping over the bottom."

"Well, we'll talk about it tomorrow," Sotla said.

Coalbrow shrugged and helped clear the table, then went to bed. She was still limping, but not badly. Gerthal and Andringir got out the chess set. Limper sat down on a stool by the fire, and Nargri settled herself at his feet. Her orange eyes gleamed in the firelight, and her grey scales shimmered. Sotla sat down on the other side of the firepit and started twisting wool into yarn. Limper watched her. Her forearms were bare. They were white, a little sunburnt on their backs. The bracelets she wore glittered as she moved her hands. Her dress was cut low enough so that when she bent to pick up more wool, he could see her breasts, which were as white as snow, and the silver chain that she wore inside her dress. There was a silver pendant at the chain's end, that rested between her breasts and glistened dully. After a while she looked over at Limper and laughed. "You're watching pretty closely, aren't you?"

"I'm still trying to remember when's the last time I saw someone as lovely as you are. There are some court ladies at Eshgorin, who were pretty good to look at. But they were dark, and I like fair women better."

"You've been in Eshgorin?"

Limper nodded.

"Is that where you got your dragon?"

"No. I've known Nargri since I was a boy, and she was a baby. Her aunt raised me."

Sotla stared at him, her mouth open. After a moment she laughed. "Some strange travelers have stayed here, but you and Coalbrow are the strangest."

Limper shrugged, then glanced at Sotla's brothers. From the look of the chessboard, Gerthal was winning the game. Andringir was staring into space and frowning, while Gerthal stared at the board. "Do you have a horse you'd be willing to sell?" Limper asked Sotla.

She nodded. "I think we can spare Rattail. Andringir, can we?"

Andringir started. "What?"

"Sell Rattail to Holrin?"

He frowned, then nodded. "I don't think Coal-brow should leave yet."

"That's her decision," Sotla said.

Limper stood up. "I'd better get to sleep."

Sotla nodded and kept working. Limper went out into the darkness and the mist, Nargri beside him.

That night he dreamt again that he was in Esh-gorin, working in the smithy. The god was behind him. He felt his presence like a fire at his back. He kept working, hammering out a blade, trying to ignore the god. All at once he felt a hand on his right shoulder. The fingers dug in, hurting him, and he felt himself being pulled around. "No!" he shouted. He woke then. For a moment he lay shaking. His right shoulder was aching and his right arm, too. He thought he could still feel those fingers, and he touched his shoulder to make sure they weren't there.

"Limper?" Nargri said.

"Nothing's wrong. I had another bad dream."

"You're getting to be a very restless sleeper."

"I am? I must have something on my mind."

After a while Limper went back to sleep. When he woke again, sunlight was shining in through the loft window. He went down the ladder, Nargri following him, and out into the sunshine. The sky was full of huge, ragged, white and grey clouds, and a cold wind blew. The green home field was spotted with shadows, that moved quickly, as the clouds that cast them were swept across the sky. Limper grinned. "It's a good day for traveling. I hope Coalbrow's feeling well."

They went over to the farmhouse. The slave-woman Stasa was out behind it, feeding the geese, and he saw Mirhav getting an armload of wood from the woodpile. There was a thin, gangling boy with him, someone Limper had never seen before. His clothes were faded and too small for him. "Who's that?" Nargri asked.

"Another slave, probably."

"Why do men enslave each other? Dragons don't do that."

Limper stopped a moment and looked at the boy. He had ragged, reddish-brown hair and a wide, pale face. "Maybe not, but when I lived in your deep home, I met plenty of dragons who were too poor to own their own tools, so they had to hire themselves out to dragons with tools."

"At least they were free."

"No one's free who has to work for somebody else and obey an employer's orders."

They went inside. Coalbrow and Sotla were there, setting plates, spoons and knives on the table. Coalbrow was dressed in boy's clothes again: brown pants, a russet shirt, and a brown belt with a plain bronze buckle. The clothes were too big for her and looked to be about Gerthal's size. "I see you won the argument," Limper said to her.

"She won both arguments," Sotla said. "She got her pants, and she's going to leave today."

"You can't," Andringir said in back of him. Limper looked around. The two brothers were standing in the doorway, light shining behind them, through the open door. "Why do you want to go with this fellow?" Andringir asked, as he came closer. "Take a look at him. A traveling smith who doesn't even own his own tools. He's so poor he has to wear other men's clothes. He's a cripple too, and from what I've seen of his work, he's not much of a smith."

Limper grabbed Andringir's shirt with both hands, swung him around and slammed him against the nearest wall. Then he twisted the shirt till it began to choke Andringir. The boy's eyes bulged, and he beat at Limper's arms. Limper let go and stepped back, hit a stool and stumbled. Andringir lunged at him. Limper grabbed up the stool and jammed it into Andringir's gut. The boy grunted and bent over. Limper glanced around. Coalbrow stood between Gerthal and the fight, a knife in her hand. Gerthal was keeping still and looking puzzled.

"That's enough of that," Sotla said.

"Plead your case with Coalbrow, if you must," Limper said. "But don't tell lies about my smith-work."

Andringir straightened up. His face was pale, and he looked sick.

"If you're going to throw up, go outside," Sotla said.

"I'll be all right," Andringir said after a moment.

Sotla went into the kitchen and came back with a bowl of porridge and a bowl of curdled buttermilk. "Coalbrow, will you go into the kitchen and get the ale and the stewed apples?"

"Holrin?"

"I think it'll be safe."

Coalbrow tucked the knife in her belt and went to get the food.

"That was a foolish thing to do, Andringir," Sotla said. "Never pick a quarrel with a man till you know him. Now you can see that Holrin is less even-tempered than you thought, and also quicker to take action."

Andringir nodded.

"I slept badly last night," Limper said. "It

usually takes more than that to make me angry."

When Coalbrow came back, Andringir said, "I'd like you to stay. I have a good farm here. I can give you more than Holrin can."

Coalbrow set the food on the table, then looked at Andringir, frowning slightly. "You don't even know what kinds of things I like."

"Most women like fine clothes—dresses with embroidery on them, fur-lined cloaks and things like that, also jewelry. I can give you those."

Coalbrow shook her head. "I like clothes I can travel in, and I've never cared for jewelry."

"What do you want, then?" Andringir asked.

Coalbrow smiled. "A sword made by the king of Eshgorin's smith."

"How could anyone buy a thing like that, unless he were in Eshgorin and had a lot of money?"

Limper sighed, then nodded. Andringir looked at him. "You can buy that for her?"

Limper hesitated, and Sotla laughed. "No wonder Holrin got mad when you said he was a bad smith. Not buy, brother. Make. Is that right?"

Limper nodded.

"Well, now I can brag that my kettle was mended by a king's smith. Set down that stool, sit down and eat."

Limper did what he was told. The others followed suit. After they'd eaten, Sotla said, "Gerthal, you and Mirhav go get Holrin's horse, and Rattail, too, and saddle them."

Gerthal nodded, then went outside. Sotla looked to Limper. "You're going to need another cloak and food as well. I'll get those. You settle the price of the horse, Andringir. But don't take less than five pieces of silver."

Limper looked over at Coalbrow. "I have that

much money," she said. "The price sounds fair to me." She got out her purse and paid the coins to Andringir.

Sotla brought them a bag of food and a thick, grey cloak. "Thank you," Limper said.

"I'm sorry to see you go. But there's no question that you're a strange fellow."

Limper grinned. "It comes of being raised by dragons."

Sotla looked down at Nargri and grimaced. "I suppose it does."

Coalbrow went and got her cloak and bow, then said, "Let's go outside."

"You go. I'll be there in a moment or two."

Coalbrow shrugged and went out. Andringir followed her. Nargri looked up at Limper. He nodded toward the door, and she hurried toward it. Sotla laughed.

"I don't like the idea of leaving without getting my hands on you at least once," Limper said.

Sotla nodded, then set down the cloak and the food-bag. "It can't do any harm, since you're leaving."

She came over to him, and they kissed. It was a pretty long kiss, and Sotla had evidently been practicing, for she had her mouth open and knew how to use her tongue. When they were done, Limper said, "I take it you have a good friend at one of the neighboring farms."

She laughed, then nodded. "Isger Whitehair. I'm going to marry him, if my mother can strike a bargain with his parents."

Limper looked down at her face. Her eyes were blue-grey, and had dark lashes. "I can't say I'm entirely happy to go."

"Never regret the inevitable, Holrin. In any

case, I could never get along with a man who keeps dragons in the house."

He kept his hands on her waist. "Your father's nickname fits you. Sunlily. If you ever get to Yara Shoi and I'm still there, I'll make you a necklace." He pulled her closer. "Lily buds. How'd you like that? Lily buds made out of gold with gold beads in between them. Or maybe the beads should be amber."

"I pity the woman you marry," Sotla said.

"Why?"

"You think about smithing too much, and women too little."

Limper felt his face grow hot. "You're right, but I don't know how you can tell."

Sotla smiled, then kissed him lightly on the lips, then stepped back. "Maybe I will come to Yara Shoi. Most likely, I'll be married soon. I'll ask Isger to take me shopping in Yara Shoi. And if we make a baby between us, you and I, it'll be easy to say it's his. Now, get going. Be sure to take care of Coalbrow. She's not as strong as she says."

Limper started for the door.

"Don't forget the food and the cloak."

He went back and got them, then went outside. Coalbrow was already on her horse. Limper picked up Nargri and set her on the other horse, a bay with a long, stringy, black tail. He tied the food-bag and the cloak behind the saddle, then mounted and looked at the two brothers. Gerthal was still looking puzzled. Andringir had a frown on his face. "Don't take it too badly," Limper said. "You and Coalbrow wouldn't have suited."

"That's something I'd have liked to find out for myself," Andringir said.

Limper shrugged, then turned his horse and rode away, Coalbrow close behind him.

He looked back once, when they reached the main road. Andringir and Gerthal were walking toward the barn. He thought he saw Sotla out behind the house, the geese all around her. But it might have been the slave-woman. He wasn't sure.

They traveled slowly, following the road northward through woods and past scattered farms. The wind kept blowing. Brown leaves whirled across the road around them. Grey and white clouds moved quickly across the sky. From time to time they saw people: men plowing the fields, a boy watching a herd of swine, a woman washing clothes in front of her house. Early in the afternoon they came to where the forest stopped and the steppe began. This wasn't the wild steppe, where nomads ranged. The road still went past pastures and ploughed fields. Here and there Limper saw chimney-smoke rising into the wide, cloudy, windy sky. They stopped at the steppe's edge to eat. Sotla had packed roast pork and dried fish, cheese, bread, and a stoppered jug that turned out to be full of ale.

"How are you feeling?" Limper asked Coalbrow after they'd eaten.

"My leg aches, but I don't feel dizzy. I'm all right."

"I'm cold," Nargri said.

"So am I, come to think of it," Limper said. He put on the cloak Sotla had given him and made sure it covered Nargri. They kept going northward, across the steppe.

Late in the afternoon they passed the last of the farms. There was nothing ahead of them except brown grassland and the blue-and-grey sky. They stopped and made camp where the road went through a shallow stream. There were bushes there and a few small trees, willows mostly

"Yara Shoi is another day's travel," Coalbrow said. "Or so Andringir told me We ought to have enough food."

Limper nodded, then set to work gathering wood for the fire. When the fire was burning briskly, he said, "Are you still planning to go north to see your father's kin?"

Coalbrow looked at the fire for a while. Finally she said, "I don't think so. They'd probably try to make me wear a dress and learn weaving. Would you mind if I stayed with you?"

"You're welcome to stay," Nargri said.

"Holrin?"

Limper nodded. "I don't mind."

"What are you planning to do?"

"Look for a job in Yara Shoi. It's time I got back to smithing. Nargri will tell you the only place I'm really safe is in a smithy Everywhere else I fall over my own feet."

"That's true," Nargri said.

"It seems to me if I find a job, the smith will do one of two things after he's seen me work: either kill me out of envy or offer me a partnership."

Coalbrow smiled "You're modest, aren't you?"

"I'm a good smith. I forget that from time to time, but it's still true."

"He is good," Nargri said. "My aunt trained him, and she's the best smith in our home "

Limper helped himself to some food. A little later, when he was finishing the cheese, he said, "What about you, Coalbrow? What do you plan to do?"

She frowned. "I don't know. I like hunting better than anything else, but I can't do that in Yara Shoi."

"Well, there's no hurry. You're still pretty young, and who knows where any of us will end up?"

"That's true enough."

After supper Limper went to sleep, wrapped in the cloak Sotla had given him. He slept badly and kept waking with part of a dream still in his mind. First he dreamed about Sotla and then about being lost in a snowstorm. He woke from the second dream shivering. The moon was up, three-quarters full, lighting the ragged clouds. The wind was still blowing, and the trees around him rustled. Coalbrow and Nargri were on the other side of the fire, sharing the second cloak. They were both asleep.

Limper lay awake till after the moon set. Then he went back to sleep and had a third dream. He was back in the smithy in Eshgorin, the god behind him. Once again the god grabbed hold of him. He shouted, "No!" But the god kept pulling him around, till the two of them were face to face. They looked at each other. The god was no taller than Limper, and his eyes weren't like fire. They were perfectly ordinary human eyes, rimmed with red because of the smithy smoke. After a moment Limper recognized the god's face. It was long and narrow with a high forehead, a high nose and light blue eyes. It was his own face.

He woke up then, rolled onto his side and looked around. He was back on the steppe, beside the river. Coalbrow and Nargri were still on the other side of the fire. Stars shone down through breaks in the clouds. A short way off the horses grazed. He could see their dark shapes moving.

"I wish you'd be a little more explicit," Limper

said to the sky. "I'm not sure I know what the dream means, if anything at all."

As usual the sky didn't answer, and Limper went back to sleep.